The Fairy Diaries

Rebecca's Quest

By Louise Bradley

The Fairy Diaries

Rebecca's Quest

By Louise Bradley

Grosset & Dunlap · New York

Library of Cataloging in-Publication Data is available

Text copyright © 2001 by Louise Bradley
Cover illustration copyright © 2001 by Broeck Steadman
All rights reserved.
Published by Grosset & Dunlap, a division of
Penguin Putnam Books for Young Readers, New York.
GROSSET & DUNLAP is a trademark of Penguin Putnam Inc.
Published simultaneously in Canada. Printed in the U.S.A.

ISBN 0-448-42493-2   A B C D E F G H I J

Table of Contents

1

Befana

My whole life, I believed something important and exciting would happen to me. I felt sure that I had to be special in some way, and that I was destined for some unique purpose. My problem was that no one else did. As it turns out, I was right, and everyone else was wrong. Of course, I can't tell anyone about my great purpose—it's top secret. It all started on the day Befana hobbled down the aisle of my school auditorium.

It was the day of the sixth-grade school play. I was onstage, playing a willow tree. Holding up a branch in each hand and standing completely still was not what I had in mind when I tried out for the play, but my teacher forgot to give me a real part, and playing a tree was all she could think of at the last minute. She was probably regretting the decision, since it was only a few minutes into the first act, and I had already dropped my left branch twice.

Standing there, I had a chance to look around the audience. Most of the seats were filled with parents. I didn't bother looking for mine. Dad picked this day (of all days!) to go to an auction of fine art objects in the city, and my mom could not miss her gardening club meeting. I was upset, but not surprised. Like my teacher (and most of my classmates), my parents barely notice I'm alive.

"Rebecca," my dad says (when he recognizes me), "be careful, or you'll be the spacebar on the keyboard of life." If that's true, then he's the dollar sign, and my mom is the percentage key. All *they* think about is money.

About halfway through the first act, I heard the door in the back of the auditorium creaking open. My heart jumped! Maybe my parents had changed their minds?

No, of course not. A tiny, shriveled-up old lady slowly made her way through the door and down the aisle toward the stage. She looked like one of those dried apple dolls you see at harvest festivals. Her clothes were really odd for a woman her age. Her dress was made from dozens of gauzy pastel scarves, and she held a cane shaped like a bird with a long neck. The strangest thing was the haze. A glowing blue haze surrounded her as she shuffled along.

She gradually made her way to the front row, where she proceeded to make a huge amount of noise.

"Excuse me! Pardon me!" she said loudly to every person in the row. "Watch your feet! My eyes aren't what they used to be, you know; I'm just an old bag of bones."

The really weird part of all this was that nobody said a word to her. No one shushed her or looked at her or even lifted their feet to let her get by. Suddenly, I felt very sorry for the old woman. I knew how she must feel, making a tremendous ruckus, and having nobody notice her. I almost wished she would whack someone with her cane to get them to give her some space! When she finally found an empty seat, the lady next to her didn't even remove the coat that she had thrown across it. The old lady sat down anyway. She settled in—then stared straight at me! I was embarrassed, and a little flattered, but mostly confused. Who was she, and why was she interested in me? After all, I was just a tree!

A few seconds later, another latecomer burst into the auditorium. He was a beefy, red-faced man, and he hurried down the aisle, his keys and loose change jingling loudly in his pockets. This time, everyone turned to look, as he rushed to the front row. My eyes (and everyone else's) followed him as he headed toward the old lady. I was afraid he would ask her to leave, but then an awful thing happened. He sat down right on top of her! I dropped both my branches and screamed.

"Mister, get off that old lady!" I yelled. He stared at me, not moving. "Please, someone help her! She'll be crushed!"

The auditorium was silent. The whole audience sat completely motionless, staring straight ahead. It was as if someone had frozen them! I jumped off the stage and ran to the front row. It was terrifying to be the only person moving in a room full of hundreds of people. Then, I saw something that made me stop in my steps. The beefy man started to rise gently up off his seat. He looked like a mannequin being lifted by an invisible crane! The little old lady jumped out from under him, as he floated six feet above the seat, in a mist of blue haze.

"Wonderful performance, yes indeed!" she said, clapping her hands vigorously. "I've never seen such a convincing portrayal of a tree! First-rate!"

I tried to say something, but the words wouldn't leave my throat.

"Are you ready to face a new challenge, Rebecca?" she asked exuberantly.

This old lady was obviously some kind of sorcerer or hypnotist. I was so afraid, my teeth were actually chattering!

"Who, who are you?" I finally managed to squeak out. "How do you know my name? Did you make everyone stop moving?"

"Ah, good. You have a questioning mind. I like that quality. And, you rushed to help me when you thought I might be in danger. Very important in your future line of work," she said, smiling.

"What are you talking about?" I asked. "What line of work?"

She seemed to understand my confusion. She sat back in the seat, with the heavy man hanging over her head in the air. It was very distracting!

"I am Befana," she began. "I come to you, Rebecca, as a messenger from the Queen of the Light Fairy Court seeking your assistance!"

Suddenly, the air smelled like flowers. A calm feeling settled over me. I suspected that I was being enchanted, but all at once I didn't really mind.

"You have talents very few possess, Rebecca," she continued. "First of all, you were born with special sight! You have the power to see fairies!"

She must be crazy. "How do you know this?" I asked incredulously. "I've never seen a fairy in my life!"

"You see me, don't you?" she asked.

"Are you . . . a fairy?" I said. She stood up. The beefy man gently descended from the blue haze back into his seat. Then I noticed something strange. I looked closely at the blue haze. It wasn't haze at all. It was thousands of tiny blue fairies, some no larger than a speck of dust, flying around his head!

2

Light Fairies and
Shadow Fairies

"Why does the Fairy Queen needs assistance from me, when she has fairies who can do real magic like this?" I asked, waving my hand toward the unmoving audience.

Befana's face became very serious. "Fairyland is divided between the Light Fairy Court and the Shadow Fairy Court. Light Fairies are born whenever something joyous happens in the human world, and Shadow Fairies are born of each evil occurrence. The Light and Shadow balance each other; too much of either would make for chaos in Fairyland and in the human world. But now, to the unending sorrow of Light Fairies everywhere, the Empress Varinka has taken control of the Shadow Court. She is an ambitious and powerful fairy. She despises humans, and wishes to destroy them."

"Why?" I asked immediately.

Befana shook her head sadly. Tears welled in her eyes. "No one knows, Rebecca. As a member of the

Light Fairy Court, she possessed strong magical powers, but at first she used them with kindness. Then *something* happened, and she turned to evil. It is one of the great and tragic mysteries of Fairyland.

"Lately, the Empress has somehow been sending members of the Shadow Court to the human world. The trouble they cause here is getting out of hand, and the more evil they spread here, the more Shadow Fairies are born in Fairyland. The balance is being disrupted. The troubles are usually small ones, for now, but the Shadow Court's every success in the human world increases Varinka's power in Fairyland, and the Light Fairy Court is very worried," Befana explained.

"What can *I* do about it?" I asked, bewildered.

"We need you to come to Fairyland and be a Fairy Finder. When you find a fairy, all you have to do is say 'We are one!' and the fairy will be instantly connected to you, so she can help you in the struggle against evil. You see, all fairies need a human to take them to the real world. Then, once they are here, the Light Fairies can use their magic to fix the evil mischief done by the messengers of the Shadow Court. There are only a few chosen humans who can find and connect with fairies. Because of your fairy sight, and your other special talent, you are one of those few!"

Now I was completely bewildered. What "talent" did I have? I wasn't strong or brave; I couldn't dance or sing or play sports. I could never even catch a beach ball, let alone a fairy! Then I thought of something.

"Is it because I'm good at finding things?" I asked.

Befana smiled serenely, and nodded. "Of course, Rebecca. To be able to find things quickly is one of the greatest gifts in Fairyland!"

I never thought of it as a "great gift." My parents think of it as my job in the family. Mom and Dad love to buy things, but they never remember where they put them. My mom will spend all day shopping for the perfect little black purse. She'll buy it, take it home, and bury it under the next fifty things she buys. A few weeks later, it's "Rebecca, have you seen my new purse?" and usually in about ten minutes, I come up with it. My dad says I have built-in radar, but my mom thinks I hide her stuff, just so I can find it for her later.

"Do you want to help us, Rebecca?" Befana took my hand. "We need you so much!"

I tried to think clearly. Here, finally, was my chance to prove that I was truly destined for greatness. But what did I know about fairies? What if the fairies ignored me, like people in the human world? What if Befana was just a strange old lady who performed magic tricks?

But in the real world I was nothing but a clumsy tree. In Fairyland, if it *was* real, I could be one of a talented few. Maybe it was time to take a chance.

I made my decision. "How do we get to Fairyland?" I asked boldly.

Befana smiled broadly, doubling the number of wrinkles in her face. "This," she said, pressing something cool and hard into my hand, "will take you to Fairyland. And it will also lead you back home, or to other enchanted places. Just say 'shut' to close it up."

Before I could say "Close *what* up?" she lifted her cane in the air, the blue haze of fairies surrounded her once more, and she vanished!

"Wait! How do I catch the fairies?" I yelled to the empty air.

I dashed out of the auditorium, as the audience slowly came to life again.

Wonder if they'll notice that I'm gone? I thought ruefully. Somehow, I thought not. I searched the school yard, but found no trace of Befana.

Cautiously, I opened my hand. In it was a heavy silver pocket watch, with a shimmering sky-blue clock face. I looked at it closely. Behind the black numbers and watch hands, I saw a tiny, perfect world turning slowly inside it! I could make out brown-and-green patches of land, dotted with lakes the size of freckles, and rivers no wider than a strand of hair. Then I thought I saw something move near one of the lakes, and I brought the watch closer, so that the tip of my nose was touching it. Or, it should have touched it. My nose didn't stop; it went right through the watch face!

Suddenly, the watch expanded in my hand, swelling up quickly, like a puffer fish. I lost my balance and pitched forward into the watch. I landed with an enormous belly flop splash, right in the freckle-sized lake.

3

Fairyland

As you might guess, I'm not much of a swimmer. Luckily, the lake was pretty shallow. When I turned to look behind me, I saw the colossal numbers of the watch face. The twelve was hanging about fifteen feet in the air at the top, and the six was touching the water at the bottom. Stepping back in the lake, I cautiously put my fingers through the center of the watch face. They disappeared! When I put my face through, I could see the school yard. The watch was my doorway back to the real world.

"Shut!" I said cautiously, and the watch closed up to its normal size. I put it in my pocket and looked around.

The lake was next to a lovely green meadow. After climbing to the top of a small hill, I could see the landscape was speckled with dense patches of wildflowers. I noticed small ponds circled with reeds and tall, dangling willow trees. A dark, forbidding forest loomed in the distance. The scene looked like a postcard my parents once sent me of the English countryside. ("Having marvelous time. Gardens here *very* disorganized. Bringing gifts. XXXOOO, Mom & Dad")

There was no trace of Befana anywhere. What was I supposed to do? How on earth was I supposed to catch a fairy? What did I do with her once I caught her? Knowing nothing whatever about fairies was a big disadvantage. Where did they hang out? How big were they? Are we talking butterfly size, Barbie-doll size, or perhaps dust speck size?

Nevertheless, I hopefully stuck my face into every flower patch and bush in the meadow. Nothing. I sat on a tree trunk by the lake to have a long think.

While I was thinking, I became aware of a buzzing noise. It was really close to my ear! I swatted away madly and stood up to make a quick escape. My hand hit something, and when I looked down to see what it was, it was looking right back up at me. And it wasn't happy.

I had accidentally slugged my first fairy. She was about three inches in height and dressed in what appeared to be a shiny pink web. Her hair was short and curly and was sprinkled with shimmering dust. Her face would have been pretty, I think, if she had not been so furious.

"You're not a bumblebee!" I said to her.

This statement did not amuse her. She pointed one tiny finger at me, and ZAP! I suddenly collapsed.

I tried to get up. But, to my complete horror, my arms and legs looked completely different. They were hard, black, and shiny, and *there were two extra of them*! Screaming was out of the question, since the only sound I could make sounded like humming. I looked down at the rest of my body. It was covered in black-and-yellow-striped fur. I felt something flapping behind me. There were wings attached to my back! The fairy had turned me into a bumblebee!

My body went rigid with panic. What was I going to do? I desperately looked around for the fairy, but she had flown away. I must be the most useless fairy catcher *ever*. Using my wings, I tried to get off my back and onto my legs. Once I was upright, I crawled miserably around looking for help.

Find the fairy, I thought quickly, *and apologize to her.*

After a few minutes of fruitless searching through the tall blades of grass, I realized that it would be impossible to find the fairy this way. Suddenly, I heard rustling in the grass. I turned to see a large lizard of some kind heading my way. I was so frightened, my fur stood on end! Was it a bee-eating lizard? Staying around to find out was not an option. I crawled away as fast as I could.

The only way out of this dangerous situation was to learn to use my wings. Then I could fly everywhere, and finding Befana or the angry fairy would be easier. I decided to teach myself to fly.

It wouldn't be easy. Even at the best of times, I'm not very coordinated. I tried running and leaping into the air flapping my wings, but that didn't work. I landed smack on my little bee face. Then I thought I would try jumping from something high off the ground. I crawled slowly up the stem of a nearby daisy. When I reached the top, I realized I hadn't reckoned on my body weight. Bumblebees are pretty heavy, compared with flowers, and the daisy started swaying precariously. Rocking to and fro, I began to feel sick, and my grip on the daisy's petals was starting to loosen. Out of sheer terror, my wings suddenly started flapping furiously. The daisy lurched backward, and I let go of the petals just before the daisy went completely over. Miraculously, I found myself hanging in midair! I was flying!

Flying gave me a whole new attitude about my predicament. With only a small effort, I could soar high in the sky or hover close to the earth. What a glorious feeling! I even flew low over the large lizard, just to show him I was no longer afraid. After a while, however, all the flying made me feel hungry. Staring down, I noticed a batch of purple flowers. Perhaps they contained nectar or pollen; but I never found out. The flowers turned out to be a trap.

Floating over a promising-looking blossom, I had the uneasy feeling that I was being watched. I turned around to check behind me, when, from the long, fluted body of one of the flowers, a hand suddenly shot out and grabbed my back leg!

"Oooo, what a lovely large thing you are!" a voice said admiringly as I struggled to get free of the hand. "That gorgeous fur will make the most divine bed-spread!" My wings flapped like crazy, but I couldn't get away.

I had been captured by a fairy! My heart sank. This was all backward! I was supposed to be catching them! The Queen of the Light Fairies certainly didn't know what she was doing when she sent Befana to recruit me. So far, I had done everything wrong, and now, I was going to be skinned by a fairy! I stopped struggling for a moment to look at my captor.

In the moment I had to look at her, I could see she was incredibly beautiful. She was a little larger than my hand (before it was bee-sized), with dazzling violet eyes and gorgeous ink black hair that cascaded over her shoulders and back. Her gown was very intricate. It was woven with bits of flower petals, corn flax, and spider-web. At first I thought she was wearing a sapphire pendant, but then I realized the blue triangle shining at her throat was actually part of her skin. (I found out later this was a special fairy charm that all fairies have, and the different symbols represent their different powers!)

Thinking that I had given up the battle, she loosened her grip on my foot. I immediately took advantage of this, and pushed myself away. Taking to the air, I flew faster than I had ever flown before. But the fairy followed me, and her wings were larger. She swooped down on me like a hawk on a pigeon. I felt her tiny hands gripping my back fur. I tried to buck her off, like a rodeo bull, but she held tight and pinned my wings against my body. She dragged me back down to earth, where I assumed the worst would happen.

4

Katrina

My whole body quaking with fear, I listened to her trying to decide how best to remove my fur.

"Perhaps a removal spell would be best for this one. My knife might tear this beautiful fur, and I do so want it in one piece," she muttered.

I felt one of her fingers poking me in the back and braced myself for the pain. It never came. Instead, I felt a kind of pleasant explosion in my body, as if I were a rosebush suddenly blossoming all at once. When I looked to see what happened to my fur, I noticed it was gone. My human body had returned! Floods of relief washed through me. But where was the fairy?

Then I noticed there was a great deal of shrieking going on underneath me. Some of it sounded like words not used in polite conversation. There was also some pinching and kicking, but I didn't get up.

"Who is that under me?" I asked, knowing very well who it was.

There was more kicking and cursing, but no reply.

"I'm not getting up until I get some answers," I said with authority.

"You hulking cow! Get off me at once, or I will turn you into the wart on a Spriggan's behind!" the little voice screeched.

That sounded awful, whatever it was. I took a chance.

"Why haven't you done it already?" I asked.

Silence.

"Are you captured now?" I was getting excited.

A really vicious pinch from beneath me told me that I had guessed correctly. Then, I remembered Befana's instructions. "We are one!" I shouted.

Slowly, carefully, I rolled off the angry fairy. She flew up into the air and swooped down again to hover in front of my face. I was fascinated by her delicate beauty. Then, she opened her mouth.

"If you believe that you can *ever* own me, you are quite wrong! I will never do your bidding! You are nothing but an ugly, clumsy, troll of a girl!" she yelled. She started flitting all around my face, throwing vicious punches wherever she could. "You were supposed to be a dazzling bedspread for the home I was planning, and then you go and turn into a completely useless human!"

Fending her off was no easy task. With my hands

now in front of my face, she tried pinching my ears and pulling hard on my hair. I started running, but she grabbed my hair and hung on.

"Ugh," she said with disgust, "your hair is like the ratty string of a hag's old shawl." She jerked on a strand as if she was playing tug-of-war with my head.

"Stop! Please!" I begged. It was beginning to hurt.

To my complete surprise, she stopped. Fluttering in front of my face again, she crossed her arms and gave me a disdainful look.

"I shall stop only when you grant me my freedom," she said calmly. Then she reached into my nostril and yanked out a nose hair.

I began to have second thoughts about the whole fairy idea. On this short visit to Fairyland, the two fairies I'd met were horrible! As far as I could see, finding fairies was a painful and dangerous activity. Catching piranhas would be easier.

Just as I was getting ready to give the nasty fairy her freedom (although how I would do this, I didn't know), I saw something large and white moving in the distance. I waved my arms in an effort to get its attention, hoping it was friendly. Whatever it was started moving toward me.

When it got closer, I was relieved to see it was not a large fairy but a young girl. She was a little older than I was, but not by more than two years or so. What I noticed most about her was her hair. It had more shades of gold, blond, and red than any hair I had ever seen. It was incredibly long and thick; it went well past her waist. At first, I thought she had a bunch of butterfly clasps in her hair. To my amazement, they turned out to be five or six small, colorful fairies. They were happily playing in her hair, making complicated braids or weaving tiny flowers, feathers, and beads in it. A baby fairy was spinning on a tiny swing dangling from the girl's ear. Yet the girl barely seemed to notice all this activity. Her eyes were huge and blue, and she was wearing a billowing white gown, with a neckline that showed off her long, swanlike neck.

She looked at me with curiosity. "Where are your fairies?" she asked.

What a strange place this was! Not hello, what's your name, but where are your fairies!

"She's . . . she's around here somewhere," I babbled, turning completely around. Nasty fairy was nowhere to be seen.

"What are those things coming out of your head?" she asked, frowning. "Are those . . . antennae?"

My stomach flip-flopped. What had the nasty fairy done? I felt my head, and gasped. Sure enough, there were two long antennae sticking out of my head: reminders of my short life as a bee.

Nasty fairy returned from wherever she was hiding. She shot out like a rocket in front of me and burst into malicious laughter.

The sound of my fairy's laughter brought out all the fairies from the girl's hair, and they all flew closer to examine my antennae. Fairy laughter is very pretty, even when it's at your expense, but this was getting ridiculous.

"Your girl is very badly put together, Katrina," one of the hair fairies said to my fairy. (Now at least I knew the name of my nasty fairy!)

"It must be wonderful to have something solid to grab onto, instead of long, beautiful hair," another giggled.

"Traveling with this human is going to be a rare treat, Katrina darling," a third said in a mocking tone. "A girl who looks like this is sure to enhance your reputation for elegance!" The other fairies broke into snide applause.

Katrina was unexpectedly quiet. As the fairy approached to touch my antennae, Katrina wheeled around and suddenly pointed her finger at my head. *Zap!* My head felt as if my hair had been yanked out by the roots. But when I felt my head, the antennae were gone! I was a normal girl once more!

5

Erica

"I'm Erica," said the girl with the hair. "What's your name?"

"Rebecca," I said, wincing and rubbing my head. "Are you a Fairy Finder?

She nodded. Then, she frowned again. "Rebecca, why did you have antennae sprouting out of your head?"

I felt ashamed. "I accidentally swatted a fairy and was turned into a bee," I admitted.

"Oh," she said, barely suppressing a smile. She thought for a moment. "How on earth did you get hold of a valuable fairy like Katrina?"

Now I felt insulted. The way she asked made it sound like it was impossible for a dolt like me to get a fairy like Katrina. I decided to change the direction of the conversation.

"What's so valuable about Katrina?" I wanted to know. "She seems perfectly horrible, if you ask me."

Erica sat on the grass and patted the ground next to her. I sat down. She smoothed down her gown and took a deep breath. I could see she was about to make a long, know-it-all speech to me. I've seen my mom do it about a million times.

"Katrina is a counter-fairy. That means she can undo any other fairy's magic, excepting the Royal Family's," Erica began. "Otherwise, only the fairy who cast the spell can undo it. Counter-fairies are extremely difficult to find, and even harder to catch."

She looked at me as if she expected me to tell her how I did catch Katrina. I kept quiet.

"Counter-fairies are also very hard to handle. They don't cooperate, and sometimes," she whispered dramatically, "may even be violent toward the Finder."

Nothing in those statements was news to me. I decided to come clean, because Erica was the only one I'd met who seemed remotely helpful. I'd just have to trust her.

"Listen, Erica," I began, "when I was a bumblebee, Katrina tried to catch me and skin me for my fur. Instead of skinning me, she undid the magic of the other fairy by mistake. When I changed back into a person, I landed right on top of her. That's how I caught her. It was all an accident, like swatting the other fairy.

So I clearly need help—can you explain this whole fairy-finding thing to me?"

Erica grinned smugly. I guess she suspected that I was a total amateur at the fairy business. "All right, I'll tell you everything you need to know," she began. "No questions until I am finished."

I rolled my eyes, and got comfortably settled for the long lecture ahead.

"First of all," she began, "you can't *make* a fairy do something. You can't even *ask* them to do things sometimes."

Erica looked quickly over at the fairies and leaned over to my ear.

"Fairies are very competitive," she whispered, "and they love to show off their powers. If one fairy sees another performing, she will try to outdo the other."

"That sounds like fun!" I interrupted. "It's like a magic contest."

"It might seem like fun," said Erica darkly, "but it can turn into a serious mess. The fairies sometimes get carried away and make much more magic than anyone needs. You have to yell "Cease!" or it could go on forever."

A thought suddenly occurred to me. "Did Katrina

undo my antennae just to show off to your fairies?" I asked Erica.

Erica nodded. I had the feeling that Katrina would never do anything for me just to be nice.

Then, I thought of something else that had been bothering me.

"If fairies need humans to get to our world, and Fairy Finders are the ones to bring good fairies there, how do the bad fairies get there?"

"Some of them are always there," Erica went on, "just as there are Light Fairies who only dwell outside Fairyland. No one knows how the Empress is bringing Shadow Court fairies into the real world."

"How do we know what the bad fairies are doing in the real world? So many bad things are done by humans, you know. How can you tell the difference? And how do you know what to do about it?"

"We get our assignments from the Light Fairy Court," she replied. "I was looking for fairies on my way there when you flagged me down."

"May I go with you?" I asked. "I still don't feel like I know what I'm doing!"

"Oh, all right," she said, with the air of a big sister who has to cart her little sister all over town. "But you'll need to catch another fairy before you can get an assignment. Katrina does not appear to be under your control enough to be helpful."

Catch *another* fairy? I'll never live to see the Fairy Court, I thought. My face fell.

"Don't worry," said Erica graciously, "I'll help you."

I sighed, and followed Erica's flowing fairy-flecked hair down the side of the hill.

6

Jenny Greenteeth

Erica led the whole band of us straight down to a grassy bank next to a pond. She commanded me to search for any clue that might lead to fairies. Looking for things! Here was something I was supposed to be good at. But this job was harder than usual. Katrina was shouting insults at me, trying to get the other fairies to laugh. Erica's fairies were no help either. They placidly decorated her hair and tried to outdo each other with the fanciness of their work.

"You said before that Katrina has the power to undo other fairies' magic, right, Erica?" I said suddenly.

"Yes," she said, poking through the grass at the edge of the pond.

"What do your fairies do? I mean, what are their powers?" I asked. "Apart from being hairdressers?"

"They're not all mine," Erica admitted. "Some of them come along just to play in my hair. They're hair fairies. Their powers are very limited. The baby here," she touched her ear, "is a Joy Fairy. He's mine. He has the power to bring happiness and contentment. Although," she put her hands around her mouth and whispered, "he finds it very hard to concentrate sometimes.

"The violet fairy over there is mine, too. She's a Power Fairy. This means she can cast a spell on something to make it do what she wants. She has power over animals."

This part of her fairy lecture was very interesting.

"Why are we looking for another fairy for me when you have extra ones?" I asked. "Can't I take one of yours?"

"That's a stupid question," she said. "Don't you think these fairies know what you're looking for? They'll protect themselves, and you'll find yourself turned into something worse than a bumblebee."

That was a good point.

After looking for what seemed like hours, I was getting sleepy. The soft meadow grass seemed so inviting, I just had to put my head down for a few minutes to rest.

Katrina flew close over my head. "The gargantuan toad is nesting by the pond, everyone!" she shouted to the other fairies, pointing down at me. "Her artful fairy-hunting efforts are done for today!"

I took a swat at her. "Buzz off, Katrina," I said sleepily.

Erica gasped. "You should never talk to a fairy that way!"

"Why not?" I asked angrily. "She treats me like dirt. Am I supposed to like it?"

"Shhh!" She dropped her voice. "They have ways of getting back at you."

I shrugged. I was too tired to care. In a moment, I fell fast asleep.

I awoke to the sound of Erica moaning, "Oh no!" I tried to get up to see what she was so upset about, and then I realized: it was me. I could not move my head. Katrina (with help from the hair fairies, no doubt) had woven my hair into the fine meadow grass so tightly that my head was fastened to the ground. With fairy laughter ringing in my ears, I struggled and pulled. Nothing worked.

"Be still, and I'll try to unravel it," said Erica.

She scraped and tugged and pulled on my hair, but weaving done by fairy hands is very tight. In the end, she had to dig up the grass in patches. I must have looked ridiculous with my hair hanging down all tangled in clumps of grass and dirt. Katrina couldn't have been happier.

Erica gave me an "I told you so" look, and I said nothing to Katrina. I stormed back to the pond to find a fairy that would do what I asked it.

After searching for a while, I found a clue. There was a furry brown pile of something near a clump of reeds. When I came closer, I saw that it was an empty sealskin. I called to Erica.

"Oooo. It's a selkie skin!" she squealed. "I thought I might find one here!"

"*You* might find! *I* found it," I said.

"Yes, but I brought you here," she pointed out bossily. "Enough arguing! A selkie skin on the side of the pond means that there is a lovely fairy in the water nearby. Once you catch a selkie without her sealskin disguise, they are very easy to handle. Very obedient."

That was all I needed to hear. I began to search the pond water with painstaking care. Soon I noticed that something was causing a ripple in the water on the other side. I sped over just in time to see a figure surface by a rock. It went back under in a moment. Edging up to the rock, I peered over.

There, under the water, was a small, green woman. No bigger than a seal pup, I thought. She was swimming gracefully, kicking her small dainty toes in the water. Then her face turned up to me, and she smiled. Her eyes were like a seal's: soft and inviting. Her delicate arms seemed to beckon to me. I reached down into the water. Her hands met mine and gripped tightly.

I heard Erica scream, "NO!" I turned at the sound of

her scream. She was running like a madwoman to my rock.

Then, I felt the pulling. I looked back, and to my horror, the lovely, sleek woman had turned into a hideous creature. She was trying to pull me into the water! I screamed and fought back, but she had a good grip. Her moldy, green teeth were showing now, and they looked razor sharp. Erica grabbed me around the waist, but the horrible creature was stronger than both of us.

Erica let go and came around to my side.

"Don't let go, she's pulling me in!" I screamed. Erica was tearing at the sleeve of my blouse. I didn't know what she was doing, but I prayed it would help.

I was almost in the water when Erica finally got the seam open. She quickly pulled my sleeve inside out.

The creature's eyes opened wide with fear. She struggled for a moment, then bit me ferociously on the arm and let go of my hands. Quickly, she vanished into the water.

Tears were streaming down my face from the fear and the pain. "Thanks, Erica," I gasped. "You saved my life!" I looked at my shirt. "What was that you did with my sleeve?"

"Magical creatures are frightened by clothing turned inside out," she explained, "and Jenny Greenteeth is no exception."

"Jenny Greenteeth? I thought you said it was a selkie!"

"A selkie would never pull you into the water! Jenny does, because she wants to drown you, then eat you."

What a cheerful thought! My stomach tightened, and I wondered about her bite.

"She almost did eat me!" I whimpered.

"Let me look at it," said Erica kindly. When I saw the look on her face, I almost passed out.

7

The Gate

ith mounting dread, I looked at my wound. One of Jenny's sharp, moss-colored teeth jutted out of my right forearm.

"Don't touch it!" warned Erica. She found a stick and picked the tooth out of my skin. It fell to the ground and quickly turned brown.

There was a big gash in my arm, but no blood was pouring out. Instead, the skin next to the hole was swelling up. A large lump was growing a bit further down. Then, something awful happened. The lump started moving.

"Uh-oh," said Erica. Her blue eyes were getting wider and wider. The fairies gathered around my arm. They were watching the moving lump with great interest. I felt a scream beginning deep in my throat, but I kept it down. The lump stopped right next to the hole in my arm.

First, we saw its little green nose. Then, its head stuck out a bit. Sensing no danger, it hopped gleefully out into my hand. It was a tiny frog, and it had hatched right there inside my arm! Even the fairies were speechless!

"I need to sit down," I said, feeling faint.

"No, come on. We have to get you to the Fairy Court. They'll fix you up," Erica said soothingly. She called out to the fairies. "To the Fairy Court!"

I staggered away from the pond beside Erica, holding out my arm, and watching. There was another lump developing, but the pain was going away. Katrina was flying right by my side.

"Mmm, what will it be this time," she wondered aloud, "perhaps a leech or a mud puppy?" She was now swinging gleefully from one of the clumps of dirt and grass in my hair.

"We'll use my portal to get to the Court," Erica said as her fairies settled in her hair. I didn't know what she meant until she pulled off her ring. It quickly grew to the size of a doorway, and we all stepped through.

By the time Erica put her ring back on, two frogs, a snake, and three newts had hopped, slithered, and crawled out of my arm. My arm was sore and slimy. Also, I was so hungry, the pond critters coming out of my arm were looking tastier by the minute.

The Fairy Court was hidden in the roots of an enormous hawthorn tree. To enter the court, Erica said, we needed to get past the gatekeeper. He was a surly, bearded dwarf holding a tall, gnarled wooden staff. He seemed to have no interest at all in letting us in.

"Oh, it's you, is it?" he said coldly to Erica, "Miss Bossyboots herself! I suppose you're in a tremendous hurry?" He sat down and lit his pipe.

"Yes, sir," Erica began politely, "you see, my friend is injured." She held out my arm, so he could see the newest snake working its way through my forearm.

"Bit by Jenny Greenteeth, was she?" The dwarf chuckled. "Have you had any newts comin' out of there? How about toads? Any big lizards?"

His interest in my swamp creatures was making me cranky. "Can we please go to the court? I can't wait much longer!"

"Ain't that a counter-fairy over there?" he said, pointing at Katrina. "Why don't you get her to undo Jenny's magic, ya darn fool girl?"

Katrina supplied the answer quickly. "This great hulking brute does not give me orders!" she shrieked, kicking the pipe out of his mouth. It didn't seem to bother him at all. He rose slowly and shuffled over to it.

While the dwarf was retrieving his pipe, four frogs, six newts, and a bright orange salamander popped out of my arm. They all stayed on the ground near my feet, looking up at me with moist and loving eyes.

"I think these animals think I'm their mother," I muttered to Erica. "They don't know I'm picturing them in a stew."

"We better get you inside," she whispered. "Gatekeeper!" Her voice took on a commanding tone. "Let us in at once! Don't make me have to speak to your superiors again!"

The dwarf scowled at Erica. As he got out of our way to let us through, I heard him mumble under his breath, "Getting me in trouble with the boss, only doing my job . . ."

As we approached the gate, the salamander darted up my leg and into the pocket of my jeans. Apparently, it couldn't bear to part with me.

When I saw the gate, I had to laugh. It was about the size of a box of cereal. There was no way Erica or I could enter it. I didn't have much time to worry about it, though. The dwarf suddenly turned and conked me on the head with his staff. When I stopped rubbing my head, I saw that I'd shrunk enough to fit through. The details on the gate were clearer to me now. It was made of some kind of polished metal. Thick vines covered the bars of the gate. Each of the wooden gateposts had many gnarled faces carved into it. And none of the faces looked welcoming.

I figured I was now about the size of a standard pencil. The dwarf had disappeared, as had the fairies. Erica was on the ground, rubbing a massive lump that was forming on the side of her head.

"That dwarf is in BIG trouble," she snarled. "I'll go straight to the Queen and report his rude behavior at once!"

"Can we stop off and get my arm fixed first?" I pleaded.

"Oh, all right," she said sulkily. Then, she said loudly, "Gate! We come to see the Fairy Queen!"

Suddenly, all of the eyes on the gatepost faces opened. Each face was different. Some were foolish-looking, with surprised expressions. Others yawned, and looked annoyed. A few looked angry and suspicious. They all started hurling questions at us at once.

"Who do you seek?"

"What is your business here?"

"What is the password?"

"What is wrong with your arm?"

"Where did you get that lovely head of hair?"

We obviously couldn't answer all their questions at the same time. Erica tried to talk, but the wooden faces started arguing about which question she should answer first.

"Well, obviously, 'What is your business here?' is the most important question," said one face to the others.

"How can you be so dim?" said the face next to it.

"The password is crucial in this situation," said another face crossly.

Another face ventured an opinion, "I think 'Who do you seek?' comes right to the point!"

"It's not 'Who do you seek," you ninny! It's *'whom do you seek'*!"

Then came screams of "You dunce!" and "Blockhead!" and "Wretched cursed idiot!" Another round of arguing got under way.

We were getting nowhere, yet again. My patience was draining out of my body. So was another frog.

"Cease!" shouted Erica, above the din. That did the trick. All faces were silent.

"Open the gate at once!" she commanded. "I am Erica, the Fairy Finder, seeking an audience with Her Highness, the Fairy Queen." All the faces looked humble at the mention of the Queen.

"The password is Tira-Na-Nog!" Erica said slowly and clearly. "Stop your arguing at once, or the Queen shall hear of this outrage!"

Erica was clearly in charge of the situation now. The gates flew open at her words. As she strode through, I heard one face whisper to another, "That one thinks *she's* the queen."

The other face replied, "She'll get hers one day." I nervously sped past them.

"Where are our fairies?" I asked Erica.

"They're not allowed in court, unless it's by invitation of the Queen," she replied, as if I should know such simple things. "Older fairies, and fairies that have performed many brave tasks are often invited. Violet has been invited twice," she said proudly. "Don't worry, our fairies are waiting for us outside by the gate."

Beyond the entrance past the gate, I heard the sound of rushing water. As we drew nearer, I saw a cascading waterfall was blocking our way.

"May the Fairy Queen rule forever!" Erica shouted.

The flowing water abruptly parted in the middle. Like the opening of a curtain, the sides began to draw apart. We stepped neatly through, onto the marble floors of a vast main entrance hall, and I got my first look at the Fairy Court.

8

The Fairy Court

It was a dazzling sight! Fairies of every shape and color were fluttering around, greeting each other gaily in that special fairy way. I'd seen Katrina and Erica's fairies do it: the fairies fly up directly in front of each other, and clasp hands gently, so as to maintain eye contact while they're in the air. They gently kiss one another's cheeks. Then, they kiss first one forehead, then the other. It's lovely, even when Katrina does it. I have no idea how they know who kisses which forehead first.

There were also insects and small animals (which of course didn't seem so small now) scurrying about the large room. Tiny elves rode the slippery backs of beetles, using the antennae as reins. A child fairy was dragging the leash of a squeaking baby mouse, trying to make it heel. Near the high, vaulted ceiling, some water sprites flying on moths were dive-bombing the harried-looking servants. There were fairy musicians practicing in one corner and dancing fairies stretching their arms and legs in another. With all the noise, I don't know how they heard Erica clear her throat, but they did. Then, the Fairy Court got its first look at me.

All activity stopped, as they stared at us. Even the salamander popped his head out of my pocket to see what was happening. In all my eleven years, I never felt so many eyes watching me. Then, a really unusual thing happened. Every single creature in the room, even some of the insects, turned to us and *bowed!* It was so amazing!

Then a squirming brown fish fell out of the hole in my arm. The whole crowd gasped.

An older fairy rushed up to me at once.

"I'm so embarrassed," I whispered to Erica. She rolled her eyes at me, and greeted the old fairy.

"Hello, Mab," she said wearily. "Here's a newcomer for you to fix up."

"Tell the kitchen elf to set two more places for the feast, Erica," said Mab.

Erica nodded and flounced off.

"No need to worry, my dear," Mab said kindly. "I'll fix you up in no time."

When Mab took my arm, the entrance hall immediately started buzzing with chatter. Strangely, even after the fish incident, everyone seemed to be looking at me with concern and respect. Mab pushed through the crowd and led me to a room off the hall. It looked like the infirmary at school. Instead of being full of medicine and pills, though, Mab's cabinet was full of bags of colored powders and jars of liquid with tiny dead animals floating in them. She carefully set me down on a vast featherbed and placed my arm in a bowl of fresh water. That was kind of her, I thought. My critters would have a place in which to swim around. They were now popping out of my arm at an alarming rate.

Feeling my head for fever, and taking the pulse on my other hand, Mab reminded me of someone. Then I remembered. It was like when my mother was tending her latest batch of seedlings from the nursery. She had the very same look on her face.

"I'll be right back with a counter-fairy," Mab said. This was probably meant to reassure me, but it didn't work.

"Please don't bring a counter-fairy," I pleaded. "I've had some bad experiences with mine."

"You have a counter-fairy, already!" she said in amazement. "That's marvelous! They're quite difficult, you know. You must have a very strong gift."

I was too weak to argue with her. "Must I have a counter-fairy?"

"It's just the thing!" she said smiling. "Cybele is a perfect darling. She'll repair this nasty bite in a moment."

She called in Cybele, who like Katrina, was tall and elegant, with a haughty expression on her face. She also had the same shining blue triangular mark on her skin. Fortunately, she did not seem to have the same distaste for me. She bowed to me courteously, and pointed at my arm.

"Wait!" I shouted. I took the salamander out of my pocket. "Will he be undone, too, when she zaps my arm?" I asked Mab.

"I'll hold him, sweetie," she said, taking him from me with a smile.

"Okay, zap away," I said nervously to Cybele. She pointed again, and I felt a pinch on my arm. When I looked, the gash was gone, replaced by a delicate, pink line that was already fading. Jenny Greenteeth's magic was undone! A flood of relief washed over me.

Mab returned to my side. "Erica tells me you haven't eaten in ages. The feast is almost starting. You'll be stronger once you have some food."

Getting up from the bed, I felt a little dizzy. Mab took my arm, and we started off to the Great Dining Hall.

"Why is everyone so nice to me here?" I asked. Unlike Erica, Mab seemed easy to question. She was open and friendly, plus she didn't have a million rules.

"Fairy Finders are like the gallant knights of King

Arthur's time. They aid Her Majesty in her battle against the Shadow Fairy Court, and they guide the lesser fairies so that they will fight wickedness and stay true to the Light Court."

Lesser fairies! Katrina would pitch a fit to hear herself described in those words.

"If the Queen is so powerful, why doesn't she fight the Shadow Fairies herself?" I asked.

"Members of the Royal Family can never leave Fairyland, and much of the evil of the Shadow Court is done in the human realm. The Queen does what she can here, but she must be protected now that the Empress Varinka gains more power each day. If anything happened to her, all would be lost!"

"Erica is a really good Fairy Finder, isn't she?" I asked Mab. She nodded.

"She has completed three tasks set for her by the Queen," Mab replied. "She is here now to receive her next assignment."

I looked at Mab anxiously. "I'll never be as good as Erica, will I?"

Mab sighed. "Lovely Erica works well with the fairies. However, she is not as skilled with the other dwellers of our world. Often they can be as helpful to our cause as the fairies. The other Fairy Finders know that, but Erica does not see it yet."

I thought about the dwarf and the gatepost faces, and silently agreed. I was about to ask how many other Fairy Finders there were, but just then we arrived at the entrance to the Great Dining Hall.

It was another gigantic room, with lavish decorations covering every inch of the walls. Portraits of fairies hung everywhere, most of them with picture frames made of twisted gold or silver. Some of the paintings showed fairies looking at themselves in pools of water. Other showed fairies facing hideous creatures of every description. Also hanging on the walls were tremendous fans made from birds' feathers of every color, and several fans made entirely of butterfly wings. The room was bright with candlelight, which gave everything a burned orange glow. There were several long tables set in a horseshoe pattern, with a space in the middle apparently reserved for the Queen. Mab let me through the room, and everyone nodded graciously to us as we walked by.

We passed a group of small, dark men in green caps who were trying to sneak bits of food off the serving dishes.

"Stop that at once!" Mab yelled at them, giving them sharp raps on the knuckles with her fists. "Imps," she said, shaking her head. "They can never wait to eat."

The food on the table smelled marvelous but was very odd-looking. There was some kind of roast in the middle of the table, but it wasn't a shape I was familiar with. There were some berries and nuts, and pitchers of what looked like milk. In front of everyone's plate was a bowl-shaped food, which I thought might be half of a grapefruit. Upon closer inspection, I found that it was something else. I decided not to ask what anything was until after I had eaten it.

I nearly had a heart attack when Mab showed me to a chair lined with luxurious black and yellow fur. A poor defenseless bumblebee had given its life so I could be comfortably seated! With tears welling in my eyes, I switched chairs with Erica, who was seated next to the empty seat of the Queen.

"Where's the Queen?" I whispered to Erica.

"She's not in Court today," she said with some disappointment. "She's on a diplomatic mission. The Queen Mother will preside over the meal."

"Where is the Queen Mother?" I asked, looking around.

Erica giggled. She pointed to the seat next to her. In it sat Mab—the Queen Mother.

9

The Dinner

"Welcome, visitors to the Light Fairy Court," Mab called everyone's attention to her. "The Queen, as most of you know, is on a diplomatic mission to the Shadow Fairy Court."

The crowd began murmuring and turning to each other with worried expressions.

"There is no need to worry, of course. The Empress Varinka cannot harm her; the Queen's magic is too powerful. When she does return, let us hope the balance of good and evil may be restored. The human world must never succumb to dark magic!"

At those words, a tremendous round of applause echoed through the hall. Only the imps didn't clap, because they were sitting on their hands to keep from picking at the food.

Mab held up her hands for silence. "As you also know, we have two visitors with us tonight from the human world." There was another burst of applause. "Erica and Rebecca, please stand up."

My face went bright red. Erica stood up slowly and

surveyed the room with a quiet grandeur. I stood up quickly and, with my typical grace and elegance, knocked my chair over behind me.

"These girls are our hopes for the future. Rebecca here has just begun her life as a Fairy Finder," said Mab, "and she has already caught a counter-fairy!"

With the next round of applause, my face went red. What if they found out how I caught her? Some "hope for the future"! My eyes darted over to Erica, who was trying very hard not to laugh.

"With their help, and the help of the other Fairy Finders, we can continue the battle against the dark forces."

With these words, Erica stood very tall and gave everyone an imperious look.

"Now, dear friends, it is time to eat! Let us all have a silent wish for the Queen's safe return." There was a moment of silence. The imps at the end of the table were practically jumping out of their seats with impatience. When Mab raised her head, everyone jumped on the food.

Servant fairies flew in from the kitchen with huge trays. I eagerly ate everything that was put in front of me. My salamander was hungry, too, so I gave him my soup. He swam around in the bowl, happily swishing his tail. His shiny head bobbed up from time to time, to gaze lovingly at me, and to make sure I hadn't left without him. I never had a pet before, but I was certain that no dog could have been as affectionate. I decided to name him Sal.

Before dessert, I asked helpful Erica what I had eaten, and, of course, she was only too happy to tell me.

"Let's start with the appetizer, shall we?" she began. "That round thing you thought was grapefruit, was a curled-up barbecued potato bug!"

She looked to see what color I had turned. I'm guessing green.

She continued. "The white liquid we drank was mouse milk, and the soup was puree of tadpole."

Gack.

"The first course—" she began.

"The one served in that spiky dish?" I interrupted.

"Yes," she said. "That was braised caterpillar, roasted in its own skin."

Double gack.

"How about that long, roasted thing?" I said, trying to keep all the food down.

"It was seared rack of chameleon," she said with relish.

My salamander turned several shades of pale and jumped back into my pocket.

I was about to excuse myself, so that I could be *really* sick, when Mab leaned over to Erica.

"Let's talk about your next mission, Erica," she said.

Erica started to pull her chair closer to Mab, when all

of a sudden there was a commotion down at the other end of the Great Dining Hall. A new visitor had arrived, just in time for dessert.

She was obviously another Fairy Finder, because the court members were making a gigantic fuss over her. I thought she might be my age, although she looked much stronger. Her arms swung confidently at her side. Smiling cheerfully at everyone, she marched up to Mab.

"The Queen sent a message that you might be needing me for something," she said as she took Mab's hands. They exchanged cheek kisses, then forehead kisses. The fairy servants brought in a chair for her, and we all sat down to finish our meal.

"Yes, dear, but first," she nodded toward me. "Annie, allow me to introduce you to Rebecca. Erica, of course, you've already met."

"Nice to meet you, Rebecca," she said, shaking my hand firmly. "I can't wait to get my next assignment! Do you know what yours will be yet?" she asked Erica.

I felt invisible again. The two of them chattered on about their different kinds of fairies and missions. After a while, Mab interrupted.

"Rebecca here has collected a counter-fairy," she said to Annie.

Annie's eyes opened wide. "Really?" she looked at me with new interest.

"Yes, tell her how you did it, Rebecca," said Erica,

wiggling two of her fingers on top of her head like antennae. I gave her a look.

"Sorry, Rebecca," Mab said, "we don't have time for that story right now." Large bowls of whipped honey pudding were being served by the servants. "It's time to tell you your assignments."

We all sat up and listened carefully.

"In the human world, there is a type of place where elders are taken to dwell together," she began.

"An old folks' home!" Annie interrupted.

"A senior citizens' center," corrected Erica.

"Yes, dear," Mab started again. "This particular one has brownies in it, who inhabited that dwelling for many years. They made life easier for the elders: cleaning, guarding against vermin, and leaving small gifts, when the mood struck them."

"Brownies?" I said in wonder. "You mean, like the Girl Scouts?"

"No, silly," said Erica tossing her mane of hair. "Little brown fairy men who live in people's houses!"

"So, what's the problem?" said Annie.

"Somehow, certain members of the Shadow Fairy Court have tricked the brownies into joining the dark side. They are now making life miserable for the elders. We need to get the brownies out of the house at once. It is a small job, requiring the magic of two fairies.

We need you girls to unite and go on this mission for the Queen."

"Do we need to unite?" asked Erica. "I already have two fairies of my own."

"Erica," Mab continued, "your fairy, Violet, has the power over animals, but for the elders to keep the animals there, the animals must entertain them. A dwelling without brownies can be very dull. Annie has the power fairy, Thalia, who can cast a spell of amusement on the animals. It is a good combination, my dears."

Erica was brooding. "My baby fairy has the power of joy. He could make the elders happy with their new pets." She fingered the little empty swing hanging from her ear.

I was beginning to suspect that Erica did not want to share this mission.

Mab pursed her lips. "Erica, you know the baby can make only one person happy at a time. We need to get the brownies out of this place and keep them out. Will you girls unite to take this mission?" she asked earnestly.

All three of us cried, "Yes!"

"Wonderful! Then I'll make the arrangements!" Mab clapped her hands together with delight, and disappeared in a flash.

10

Leaving Fairy Court

"How are we getting there?" I asked Erica as we left the Great Dining Hall.

"*You* are definitely *not* going!" she said, stomping into the corridor.

Annie was trying to keep up with Erica. "Why can't she go?" she asked Erica, puffing.

Erica pulled Annie quickly ahead, presumably so that she could tell her about my adventures with fairies thus far. I followed behind, feeling miserable. There was no chance that I could be useful to the Light Fairy Court unless my fairy helped on this mission. Yet, the thought of Katrina helping was too ridiculous to think about. She would probably undo all the good magic out of pure spite.

When I finally caught up to Annie and Erica, it was too late. Annie spoke first.

"Erica's right. You cannot go on this mission with us," she said firmly. "It's dangerous to involve a girl who does not have good control of her fairy."

She sounded as if she was quoting some rule book. Or Erica.

"Annie, I don't know what Erica's told you, but I know I can help you on this mission! Please, please let me come!" I begged.

"How?" asked Erica nastily. "How could you help?"

I had to admit, inside myself, that I had no idea. Then, Mab reappeared.

"Rebecca, do you live near a village called New York?"

Some village, I thought. "Yes, it's not very far from my house," I said. "Why?"

"Splendid!" she cried. "The three of you can use Rebecca's house as a base of operations. What is your portal, dear?"

At first, I didn't understand what she meant. Then, I remembered the watch face.

"It's a watch," I said.

"Good," said Mab. "Think of home when you step through it, and it will lead you there."

"Isn't there any other way to get us to New York, Mab?" Erica asked.

"No. Neither of your doorways leads anywhere near the elders' home," said Mab. "To go on this mission will be good practice for Rebecca."

Erica and Annie sulked. They were stuck with me, and they knew it.

"Good luck, girls!" said Mab with a smile. "I know you'll get those brownies out of that house! Rebecca here is going to be a great help!"

Suddenly, I felt guilty. I asked Mab if I could talk to her alone.

When we were out of earshot of the other two, I said, "I don't know if I'll ever be a real Fairy Finder. Erica knows the truth about me. She knows I only caught the counter-fairy by accident. I have no control over her at all!"

To my surprise, Mab grinned. "I know all about you and Katrina. Erica told me everything while you were having your arm repaired."

Leave it to Erica to tattletale.

"A counter-fairy cannot be commanded. But she can help on missions in important ways. Make her comfortable, be gracious to her, let her have her way for a while, and she'll learn to respect you. I still believe that you have the gift, Rebecca. Sometimes what seems like an accident is really your power showing itself in a mysterious way."

I felt so happy, I almost cried.

Mab led the three of us down a long, narrow staircase. We entered a dark room, with a glistening pool in the middle of it. Mab's voice echoed as she spoke.

"Rebecca, this is the exit from the Fairy Court. Annie and Erica, please make sure Rebecca gets hold of a good, swift water sprite, because this is her first time. Good-bye, girls, and I hope the Queen will be here upon your return!"

Then she pushed me into the pool.

11

Annie's Fairies

As I splashed into the pool, I felt Annie and Erica jump in right behind me. I opened my eyes underwater to see two sleek, green fairies heading straight for me. After my Jenny Greenteeth experience, I was more than nervous about this. Panicking, I turned to swim away, but they soon caught up. Each one grabbed me under my armpit, and we sped off through the water.

Erica's water sprite took her by the hand, and Annie's held fast to the belt on her pants. I was embarrassed to need two sprites. We all got to the end of the pool, and the sprites pushed me up over the water.

Annie's head popped up. "Take a nice deep breath, Rebecca, because we're going to be underwater for a while."

"How long is a while?" I shouted, as her head disappeared under the water.

Erica's head came out of the water for a moment, but that was apparently all she needed. She went back under and was gone.

I took a huge breath, then nodded to my sprites. I hoped they knew what they were doing. We dove down deeper and deeper, until I didn't think we could get back up before I would drown.

Swimming with water sprites is faster than holding onto the back of a dolphin. It's more like holding on to a torpedo. We cut through the water so quickly that I barely had time to open my eyes. When I did, I saw that we were swimming up to an underwater cave. I couldn't believe that they could see where they were going, but then I noticed that their eyes shone like bright green lanterns in the dark cave. They suddenly turned upward, and, in a moment, my head was above water. I started greedily gulping air, and waited for the others. Sal jumped out of my pocket and swam merrily around my head. He probably wanted to go for another speed swim with the sprites.

Erica and Annie arrived a moment later.

"That was the fastest sprite I've ever had!" cried Annie.

"She wasn't that fast, Annie," said Erica. "Mine got to the cave first."

"Yes, but we passed you in there," Annie crowed.

"Well. That doesn't matter," said Erica quickly. "At least Rebecca didn't drown, miraculously enough."

We swam to a grassy bank near a familiar-looking hawthorn tree. There, we met our fairies. Annie's fairies starting whooping for joy when they saw her. They seemed like such a happy little family. Erica's fairies immediately started working on her very wet hair. The baby fairy, gurgling with delight, took his place under her ear.

My fairy, however, looked spitting mad.

"Where have you been, you great sow of a girl!" she roared.

I looked at her in astonishment. "You know exactly where I was, Katrina!" I snapped. Then I remembered Mab's words, and I changed my tone. "Did you miss me?" I asked as sweetly as I could.

She answered by vigorously slapping the tip of my nose. Nothing changes, I thought unhappily.

The happy little family idea did not seem possible with Katrina. She looked down upon Annie's fairies.

"Those fairies are happy to be slaves," she said disdainfully. She didn't like Erica's fairies much either. "The way they fuss over that hair is ridiculous," she sneered. Every once in a while, though, she flew over to tickle Erica's baby fairy.

Before I pulled out my watch, Erica took me aside.

"Will your parents think it's weird that you're bringing home two complete strangers?" she asked.

I hadn't thought about that at all. They would probably faint if I brought someone home with me.

"How long does time take in Fairyland compared with the human world?" I asked her.

"A few days in Fairyland," she said, "are only a few seconds in human time."

"Whew, that's a relief," I said. "They're out for the day. We'll have the whole house to ourselves."

"Great," said Erica. She then assumed a commanding tone to the rest. "Hold hands as you step through the face of the clock. If we don't, it might close up before all of us go through," she said. "Fairies, grab onto your girl's ear."

"Does the goosenecked, hairy creature never tire of giving orders?" asked Katrina in my ear. I smiled. It was the first thing Katrina and I had ever agreed on.

12

Katrina's Home

ne by one, we stepped into the watch face. I stepped out last. "Shut!" I said loudly, and the watch shrank down quickly and dropped into my hand. I stuffed it in my pocket. When I turned to Erica and Annie, they were both staring at my house with their mouths hanging open.

"*That's* your house?" gasped Erica. "It's huge!"

"It looks like the president should live there!" said Annie. "What's it like inside?"

I led the way, and they were even more impressed when they saw all my parents' expensive furniture and knickknacks.

Showing them around, I realized that my family was pretty rich. This might sound strange, but I never thought about it much. Annie and Erica settled in the kitchen and proceeded to eat all the human food they could find. Violet and Thalia gorged themselves noisily on a bowl of cherries. Annie's other fairy, Brianna, and Erica's baby fairy curled up like kittens on a soft cushion in the living room and slept the whole time we were there.

I filled my mom's crystal punch bowl with water and put Sal in it.

Most delighted with my house was Katrina. Her eyes lit up at the sight of it all. I never saw her fly around so quickly! She touched and caressed everything that was valuable (which was nearly everything). Terrified that she would break something, I tried to distract her into conversation. Mab's voice rang in my ears. Make her comfortable, she said. Be gracious.

"Katrina! Is there anything I can get for you?" I said, trying to sound polite.

She eyed me doubtfully. "What could you possibly do for me? That is, unless . . ."

Sensing that she was weakening a little, I jumped in. "Unless what?"

"You could give me your house," she said casually.

I suppressed the urge to scream at her. "Katrina, I can't do that. The house doesn't belong to me. It's my parents' house."

She glared at me with utter contempt. "What can you do for me then, you lumpish—" she began.

"Wait, Katrina!" I interrupted. "I have an idea. There's a whole bunch of stuff in the attic that's just as nice as the things down here. You can have anything from there that will fit in a fairy-sized home. I even have a fairy-sized house upstairs in my room. Do you want to see it?"

Katrina could not resist. The idea of a house of her own was too entrancing. She let me show her the way up the stairs.

What I had in mind for her was my old Barbie Dream House. It was just the right size, and had furniture in it as well. Unfortunately, it did not appeal to Katrina at all.

"That horrible pink thing! You cannot be serious! What is it made of, painted eggshells? Dried toad skin?"

"It's just plastic, Katrina," I said, trying to be calm.

"Plastic! I cannot live in plastic," she wailed. With a mighty kick of her strong little legs, she toppled the Dream House. Wheeling around, she suddenly spied my bookcase. "Is this real wood?" she asked, running her hand over it.

"One hundred percent mahogany," I said. "My mother says it's the finest wood in the world."

At these words, Katrina's eyes lit up again. She started pulling all my books off the top shelf. Soon she was flinging them happily all over the room. It made quite a racket, and Erica and Annie stopped eating to call upstairs and ask if everything was all right.

"Don't worry," I shouted down to them, "we're just redecorating!"

In a few minutes, Katrina had cleared the shelf.

"Now," she said, rubbing her delicate hands together, "where are these beautiful attic things?"

I took her up to the attic. We found an empty box, and Katrina set out on a treasure hunt through the attic. Or rather, she sent me out on a treasure hunt for her. She shouted out a kind of laundry list of things she needed for her house, while I searched for what she wanted and brought it to her box. Then she'd think of something else that was "vitally necessary." It became a kind of game with us. Before long, she was trying to think of things I couldn't possibly find. Yet, somehow I did find them, and when I brought them to her, she seemed honestly delighted.

We brought everything down to my room. "Now, be gone," she said bluntly. "I must make my house in my own way."

That idea made me a little nervous, but I left her alone.

As I came down to the kitchen, I heard Erica and Annie planning their strategy. They were saying that the house we were going to de-brownie was in Brooklyn. There was an animal shelter not two blocks from the house. They would need to go there first to enchant the dogs and cats. When I came into the room they changed the subject to more mundane matters.

"Can you buy us the train tickets to get to this place?"

Annie said in her direct way. "Erica and I don't have any cash with us."

"Sure," I said quickly. I picked up the phone and charged the tickets to my dad's credit card. Then I ordered a car service to pick us up.

Suddenly a thought occurred to me. "Don't you guys have to call your parents or something?"

Annie and Erica exchanged a look.

"Both my parents are gone," said Annie quietly. "I live in a group home, and they don't really keep track of me. I just go back every once in a while, so they don't get suspicious." She turned to Erica.

Erica thought a long time before answering. "My family isn't expecting me for a while," she said finally. "We have plenty of time before I have to go back there."

"Rebecca!"

I heard Katrina's little bell-like voice calling me from upstairs. She had never used my actual name before. This seemed like a very positive sign!

"Rebecca, come forth! Bring Gooseneck and the Slave-Driver with you!" she called. Erica and Annie did not seem amused with their new nicknames.

All of us, including the other fairies, went up the stairs. I must admit, I was nervous about what I might find.

Katrina's bookshelf house was the most luxurious

little place I had ever seen. She was sprawled across her new bed, which was made out of a gem-encrusted jewelry box and a mink beret. Its bedspread was a satin evening glove. She had used tiny, crystal perfume bottles as vases for the flowers she took from the garden. For chairs, she "borrowed" several pieces from my mom's antique pincushion collection. Hanging from her "ceiling" like chandeliers were necklaces and bracelets made from diamonds, rubies, and emeralds. A mixture of silk and velvet scarves covered the floor. Every wall was covered with mirrors.

The wings of Annie's and Erica's fairies flapped furiously. Their skins were actually turning slightly green!

"Wow!" Annie exclaimed. "Katrina, that is amazing! Where did you get all that stuff?"

Mostly from my mom's room, I guessed. She used some of the things from the attic, but she must have found her way to where the real treasures were hidden. Luckily my mom has no idea just how much stuff she owns, so I hoped she wouldn't notice.

"It *is* quite nice, isn't it?" Katrina drawled lazily, looking directly at Annie's Thalia and Erica's Violet. They folded their arms, and fiercely flapped their wings. Katrina beamed. She gazed at herself in one of the mirrors and started combing her hair. I noticed she was using my father's solid gold mustache comb.

"You have to be careful, Rebecca," Erica warned me.

"Once fairies find a mirror, it's very hard to get them to stop looking at themselves."

The other fairies giggled, but Katrina wheeled around and looked at Erica in a fury. She pointed her finger at Erica's hair. *Zap!* All of Erica's beautifully woven braids came undone; the beads, flowers, and feathers falling to the floor in a heap.

Now Violet was angry, since it was her handiwork Katrina had undone. "I think your house is ridiculous, Katrina. My girl would never allow anything so . . . so obvious!"

Thalia spoke up. "If Katrina was gracious, she would share with us. It's very *selfish* of you, darling, to have all this for yourself!"

Those were the words that started the fight. Soon, there were wildly flapping wings, tiny hurling bodies, and vicious oaths and curses flying all over the room. We humans decided to beat a hasty retreat. I closed the door to my room and hoped I could contain the damage there.

"Katrina is very difficult, isn't she?" asked Annie.

I smiled. "I think we're starting to get comfortable with each other."

13

Brownies

The battle raged on for about ten minutes. Toward the end, we heard loud banging sounds. "They can't kill one another, can they?" I asked worriedly.

Erica yawned. "No, let them fight. Any magic they do to each other, your Katrina is sure to undo." Then her voice lowered conspiratorially. "Oh, and you might want to take down that little house before your mother sees it. If your parents ever see Katrina's magic, she would have to return immediately to Fairyland."

I nodded, but silently thought to myself that the odds of my mother actually going into my room were small, and that Erica was even a little jealous of Katrina's beautiful house.

Then the racket upstairs finally died down, and I opened the door to my room. I got quite a shock. There were books everywhere (including outside on the back lawn, I found out later). My mahogany bookcase now looked like a luxury apartment building. Thalia had set up house under Katrina's shelf, and Violet was on the bottom shelf. More of my mom's belongings were pilfered, I noticed. Flowers from her precious garden adorned every shelf. The fairies were blissfully happy, and I really didn't care about the things they took. A small part of my bedroom now looked even prettier than the Fairy Court.

After the car service arrived to pick us up, everything went like clockwork. We took the train to New York and grabbed the subway to Brooklyn. Thalia and Violet were horrified by New York; all the noise and the machines were too much for them. They tucked themselves away in pockets. Katrina, however, sat right on my shoulder and watched. Fortunately, no one could see her or hear her insulting opinions on everyone and everything. Erica received some startled glances, since she was still wearing her flowing white gown. On the subway, she really looked like a creature from another planet! We arrived in Brooklyn and found our way to the animal shelter.

The back of the animal shelter was a chain-link fence. I was worried that we couldn't get the dogs and cats out of their cages.

"The fairies can make anything fly. Violet can lift the animals up and over, as long as they're outside," Erica explained. "Annie, you and Rebecca go to the senior citizens' home. We need to make sure the brownies are taken by surprise, or they might mount a counterattack."

We ran the two blocks to the house. It was a large, old-fashioned house, with ivy-covered walls. There were plenty of windows to peek into, so Annie and I ran around the back. We each stood on a garbage can and looked inside.

The room we saw was apparently the main room, because there were about ten or eleven older people gathered in it. It was a complete mess! The two women working there were trying to keep things neat, but as soon as they'd put something away, something else would get messy. They were scratching their heads in puzzlement. They must have thought the old people were doing it on purpose. But we knew the reason the room would never be clean. Annie and I could see the brownies.

At first, they were hard to see, even for us. They darted around the room, pushing glasses of juice over, opening bottles of pills and spilling the contents, and turning the pictures hanging on the wall upside down. Worse than the mess they made was the way they tortured the old folks. We saw the brownies pulling hair, putting chewing gum on wheelchair wheels, and playing with the volume control on one poor man's hearing aid.

Annie was practically in tears, she felt so bad for them. Thalia looked determined. Katrina, on the other hand, was admiring the nail polish she had chosen from my mom's manicure kit. Then, we heard the marching.

First, we saw Erica leading the way. Violet flew behind, making eye contact with the subjects of her enchantment. The dogs and cats were lined up beautifully, two by two, marching like soldiers. It was a very strange sight, but I had to admire Erica's skill in getting Violet to use her magic properly.

"Violet did her part perfectly!" said Erica proudly, while Violet marched the animals around the back.

"Wait until Thalia gets her turn," said Annie defensively. Thalia looked as if she couldn't wait much longer.

It's not just fairies who get too competitive, I thought to myself. I was glad to be a mere spectator at this point.

We all went back to looking in the window. The brownies were getting out of hand. They started a food fight with the rice pudding the old people were having for a snack. The two attendants threw up their hands and stormed out of the door. This was our opportunity.

Erica opened the back door. The dogs and cats filed in quietly. The brownies, however, were not so quiet. They screamed like banshees, although only we could hear them. In their rush to get out of the house, they began to crash into each other. The scene was very funny; with the dogs and cats sitting quietly, the senior citizens staring at the dogs and cats, and the brownies bouncing off each other in their efforts to escape.

Finally the brownies had all fled the building. We saw them escape down a hole in a little mound in the yard. Annie, Erica, and I started cheering. Some of the dogs and cats started helpfully licking up the rice pudding. Others went placidly over to the senior citizens. Thalia flew dramatically to the middle of the room and started pointing her finger all over the place.

First, a little dog jumped up on his hind legs. The man in the wheelchair smiled cautiously. Then, a small cat on the other side of the room used its tail to tickle the arm of the woman whose lap she was seated on . The woman laughed and pet the cat. Soon, all around the large room, the dogs and cats were doing small tricks to amuse the old people. Everyone was smiling, petting, or laughing. It was a happier place now.

For a short time, anyway.

Thalia was radiantly happy. She flew over to Annie, who was also thrilled with the success.

"Thalia did *her* job magnificently!" Annie said loudly.

Katrina laughed. I thought it was funny, too, the way Annie and Erica went on and on about their fairies. One of them was always trying to get the last word, although we were *supposed* to be working together.

Thalia was furious. She thought Katrina was laughing at her. That's when things got ugly.

14

Animals Enchanted

"Katrina!" Thalia sputtered indignantly, "I take a few measly dogs and cats, turn them into brilliant performers, and all you can do is sit there and laugh!"

Katrina started to speak, but Violet interrupted.

"What do you mean a 'few measly dogs and cats'?" stormed Violet. "That is a perfectly trained army of animals!"

"Dogs and cats? The dullest beasts of the human world! Only *I* can make them interesting!" Thalia cried, and flew to the center of the room again. She spun like a top, pointing her finger and zapping.

Abruptly, the animals became experienced circus performers. Dogs danced on their toes. Cats were yowling in harmony together, their tails swishing in time to the music. A cocker spaniel was doing back flips over the furniture. The old people loved it. They were applauding like mad.

This made Violet even angrier. She decided to make

it a little more complicated. I heard a clumping up the back steps and turned in time to see a riderless police horse going up the stairs, followed by a herd of earthworms and about fifteen squirrels. I turned to Annie and Erica in alarm.

"Tell the fairies to stop!" I yelled. Katrina was whooping with laughter on my shoulder. Erica's baby fairy was giggling, too.

Annie and Erica tried. They were yelling "Cease!" until their throats were sore, but they couldn't be heard.

Thalia was having a ball. She had the police horse singing love songs in Spanish. The squirrels were performing a very strange ballet that looked like "The Nutcracker." The earthworms were trying to entertain everyone with their version of the hangman game, in which they formed the letters of the alphabet with their bodies. The senior citizens, who thought they were losing their minds when the brownies were torturing them, were certain that they were senile now.

"This is all your fault!" Erica shouted at me. "Katrina shouldn't have laughed."

"*My* fault!" I yelled back. "I didn't do anything!"

Katrina was still laughing. She turned to Erica, and said, "You and Annie have such wonderful control of your fairies! It's quite entertaining!"

I turned to see a policeman running toward us down

the street, clearly looking for his horse. He heard the incredible amount of noise and headed straight for the house. I tried to get Erica's attention, but she was too furious with Katrina.

"At least our fairies don't just sit around admiring their own reflections night and day!" she screamed.

That did it. Katrina pointed and fired a huge *ZAP* into the crazy room. As the policeman reached the last step, and opened the door, all the magic stopped. The dogs and cats were back at the shelter, the earthworms back in the ground, the squirrels back in the trees, and the police horse whinnied for his master down the street. The policeman looked at us, shrugged, and chased after the horse. The old people looked like survivors of a small tornado.

Tears were streaming down Annie's cheeks. "We failed!" she cried miserably. "It was an easy job, and we blew it."

15

Emergency

I felt terrible. While I didn't think the mess was my fault, I still really wanted Annie and Erica to help the old people. It was too dangerous to try the magic again with the policeman trotting around the neighborhood. There was nothing to do now but return to Fairyland. As we went out of the backyard, I thought I spotted a brownie peeking out of the hole in the mound to see if the coast was clear. That made me feel even worse.

Erica took off her ring and cried, "Back to the Fairy Court!" One by one, we stepped through her ring.

The dwarf sat at the gate, sleeping. Erica shook him roughly to wake him up.

"Get to your feet and let us in this minute!" she said angrily.

The dwarf got to his feet slowly, looking annoyed.

"If it isn't Miss Bossyboots! Here again so soon?" he said, stretching his arms. He noticed Erica's angry expression. "Did you triumph over the brownies?" he asked, with a teasing note in his voice.

Erica stamped her foot. I never saw her look so

incensed. Annie and I looked at each other and decided to take a different approach.

"Can the Queen receive us today?" Annie asked the dwarf politely.

"Please, sir, we need to tell her about our mission," I added.

The dwarf's face softened a little. He leaned closer to Annie and me. "I'll let you two in, but that bossy one stays outside."

I suddenly felt sorry for Erica. She was having a really bad day, and the dwarf was enjoying making her miserable.

I whispered in the dwarf's ear. "That girl may be rude, but she's a wonderful Fairy Finder. One day, she'll help defeat the Empress Varinka. Mark my words."

At the sound of the Shadow Fairy's name, the dwarf shuddered. "I guess we are all working for the same thing," he said hurriedly. "Just tell her to mind her manners, all right?" He took his staff and tapped all three of us gently on the head. I saw the gate ahead of us and remembered Erica's last encounter with it. I whispered quickly to Annie.

Annie jumped out in front and went over to the gate. She started singing a song I never heard before, in a language that was completely unfamiliar. The heads carved into the gateposts opened their eyes and smiled. Erica folded her arms impatiently.

"Speed it up, Annie," she said loudly.

The gate faces scowled, but Annie continued her song, ignoring Erica. The song ended with the words 'Tira-Na-Nog,' and the gates flew open.

"Excellent performance" and "Well done!" the heads were saying to Annie. We walked right through. The gates started to close before Erica was all the way in, and she had to run before she was closed out.

Shouting "May the Fairy Queen rule forever!" to the waterfall, we charged into the Main Entrance Hall. It was completely empty.

"I don't like this one bit," said Annie warily as we searched for court members. Then, we heard noise coming from the Great Dining Hall. We dashed over and saw a figure near the back of the room.

It was Mab, and her face was very grave. She saw us and waved us in.

"I'm sorry, Mab," Erica said as she walked up. "We didn't—"

"Erica dear, don't worry about the brownies," Mab broke in. "The Light Fairy Court has temporarily dispersed. While the Queen was on her mission of diplomacy, she uncovered a terrible plot. The Empress Varinka is planning to kidnap a child born with the gift!"

The three of us gasped. Did this mean that she was coming after one of us?

Mab continued. "The Queen reasons that the Empress Varinka dare not come after any of you, with your powerful fairies to protect you. However, there is a baby, born six months ago, who has the gift. That child will be the target!"

The Shadow Fairy Court was much worse trouble than I had imagined.

"If Varinka succeeds, this baby will grow up to be her slave. The child will have all the powers of a Fairy Finder, but she will use those powers for evil. The Empress will use the child to bring more and more dark magic into the human world. Her power will be so great, that even our good Queen will not be able to vanquish her.

"We believe that Varinka will send a Spriggan to do the horrible deed. I will need one of you to defend the baby against this attack."

A Spriggan? What on earth is that? I wondered.

"The plan is simple. One of you will bring the baby back to Court, so that the Queen can perform an enchantment of protection upon her. Which of you is prepared to save this child?"

Every hand shot up. Mine was the first one in the air.

16

The Spriggan

"You are all brave girls," Mab declared with a smile. "The girl who is chosen will come with me so I can explain her task. The other two, find as many fairies as you possibly can. The Queen is marshaling her forces as we speak. If the Spriggan gets to the baby before we do, it means we must do battle with the Shadow Forces!"

That statement gave everyone a good scare. Yet, in the back of my mind, I was thinking that I'd rather do battle with an army of Spriggans than face collecting another fairy.

Mab took a few moments to make her decision. I didn't think there was any chance that she would pick me for such an important job.

I was right. She chose Annie. No surprises there, but I felt disappointed. Erica, however, was completely devastated. She pulled me aside.

"If I'd done well on the last job, she would have picked me for this one," she moaned.

That didn't make sense, because Mab chose Annie. I, however, did not say this to Erica.

I turned to say good-bye to Annie and to wish her good luck. She was on her way to meet her fairies.

"This is the opportunity I've been waiting for," she said enthusiastically. "Brianna's shield of protection has always worked for me, and it's definitely strong enough so that no Spriggan can get past! All we really have to do is go to the baby's room, shield her quickly, and come back here. It's a piece of cake. We'll just have to make a quick escape, or the baby's parents will hear us."

As Erica and I made our way to the exit pool, I asked her to tell me about Spriggans.

She went into lecture mode. "A Spriggan is a small goblinlike creature. He is hideously ugly, and although he's small, he can make himself large very suddenly. He greatly fears clothing turned inside out and fresh pond water."

I suddenly thought of something else. "How does Annie get into the real world?"

"You know how you have a watch face to take you to the human world? Annie has a picture frame. The baby's room is enchanted, so it can take them there instead of to Annie's house."

"How do you know all these things, Erica?" I asked.

"I spend a lot of time in Fairyland," she said. "You pick things up."

Erica and I jumped into the pool, and the sprites took us on another wild ride. (I only needed one this time!) When we got up on dry land, the fairies were all over us, asking questions. Even Katrina wanted to know what was going on.

Erica reassured everyone. "The job will be one of protection. If Annie uses her fairy's magic properly, the job should be simple." She said this matter-of-factly, but she had a strange look in her eyes.

She turned to me. "I'm sorry if I said some mean things to you, Rebecca. If you can believe it, I was trying to help. Please don't be insulted, but I'd rather travel alone from now on."

I was really shocked. Alone, without Erica in Fairyland? I probably wouldn't last an hour. But I couldn't bring myself to ask her to stay with me. Asking her for a favor was too difficult.

We parted with a short hug. I waved until I couldn't see her anymore. Katrina was not at all sentimental.

"Free at last from Gooseneck!" she cried triumphantly. "Let us return to my lovely house in the human realm."

"No!" I said at once. "I have to collect more fairies. Mab said I must."

Disappointment spread across Katrina's face. "But you have no talent for it! Why do you persist?" she asked.

I had no answer for her. We traveled along, not speaking to each other, until we came to a tiny pond.

It looked much too small to house anything really dangerous, thank goodness. I poked around the reeds, looking for clues. Katrina settled on top of a lily pad near the edge. I started thinking about how Annie caught fairies. If I used my talent for finding things to find fairies, it might work. When I'm looking for something for my mom, I go to where she was last and sit there. I listen. I smell the air. I get down on the floor. I move my eyes over every inch of the room. If it's not in that room, I move to another.

Why not use the same technique to find fairies? Katrina watched me with interest. I must have looked like a cat stalking its prey. I sat looking at the pond for what seemed like hours, although it was probably only ten minutes. Then I heard the splashing.

It made a very delicate sound. If I had walked around the pond, I wouldn't have heard it. In the stillness, it sounded like a small fish. I stared at the direction of the splashing sound. A flash of yellowish green leaped out of the water for less than a second, then disappeared back under. It looked like a tiny sprite. I waited to see it again. It flashed by in a second and was gone again. She swam closer to me the next time she jumped, and I could see it was a fairy. Her wings were pinned back, and she had a sleek body, smaller than Katrina's. If I could guess where she came up next, I could probably catch her.

I thought about it carefully. The fairy seemed to be swimming in a circle. She shot by again. I slowly put my hand out to where I thought she might be next. She jumped. I closed my hand quickly. Her wings were fluttering frantically in my closed fist. I put my other hand on top to give her room to move.

"Katrina! Look!" I whispered excitedly. Katrina flew over. She seemed only mildly interested in my triumph.

"Are you quite sure it's a fairy?" she asked mischievously.

Now I wasn't so sure.

"What else could it be?" I asked nervously.

Katrina reeled off the longest list of horrible pond creatures she could name. I was getting really worried.

So worried that I did a really stupid thing. I forgot to say, "We are one."

I opened my hand. The yellow-green fairy took one look at me, laughed, and dissolved into a pool of water. The water slipped through my fingers, making a puddle near my feet.

Katrina, as usual, found it very amusing. "One pond creature I forgot to mention, the Asrai. That's the fairy you let slip through your fingers." She turned to the puddle. "Come here, darling."

The other fairy materialized out of the puddle. She flew over to Katrina, and they exchanged kisses.

"Merridie! Come and meet my girl! She longs to capture fairies, but the art is lost on her," Katrina laughed.

Merridie floated inches from my face. I knew I couldn't catch her now, and the frustration was unbearable.

"Katrina," she said in a voice so high I could barely hear her, "does your girl know about the baby?"

"Yes, I've heard," I said softly.

Merridie burst into tears. I had never seen a fairy crying before. "The poor little thing," Merridie wept. "What if the Spriggan should take her? How terribly sad!"

Unbelievably, Katrina's eyes were also welling up with tears. Soon, they were sobbing on each other's shoulders and making quite a racket. A few other curious fairies came fluttering up, and they, too, joined in the outburst. Two of the fairies looked very familiar.

"Katrina!" I said, trying to get her attention. "Aren't those Erica's hair fairies?"

Katrina broke away sniffling from Merridie's shoulder. She looked at the other fairies and nodded.

"Ask them what happened to Erica!" I said. She looked at me in disbelief. "Please!" I implored.

She flew over and asked. When she flew back, her face was serious.

"They say that Erica has gone to try and get into the human world to protect the baby from the Spriggan."

17

The Baby

Would Erica do something as foolish as that? I asked the hair fairies where exactly she was, and they said she had returned to the palace. I used my watch face to get there, with Erica's hair fairies clinging to my hair (and bemoaning its lack of color and thickness) and Katrina and Merridie each grabbing an ear. We caught up to Erica near the entrance of the palace. The dwarf was snoring loudly, and she was having no luck awakening him.

"It's wrong, Erica," I cried. "Mab said only Annie should go!"

"What if *she's* wrong?" said Erica, turning on me angrily. "What if something happens, and she can't fight the Spriggan? It would be terrible for the poor baby!"

The fairies all burst into a new round of tears.

Suddenly Violet flew up, her wings flapping with agitation. She pointed toward the sprites' exit pool. There, before us, stood a picture frame. It was about ten feet high and about six feet wide. It was Annie's entrance into the human world. Erica and her fairies made a dash for the frame. Katrina, Merridie, and I tried to catch them.

I managed to grab hold of Erica's hair just as we popped through the frame. We all tumbled right into the middle of the baby's room. Erica looked at me with anger flashing in her eyes, but she said nothing.

Annie's picture frame was still standing in the room. It had a picture of a handsome man on it. For a moment, Erica stared at the picture. She looked completely bewildered.

The fairies were all hovering over the crib. With relief, I saw the baby sleeping in it. But where was Annie? Why was her portal left open? Erica peeked over the top of the crib. She reached down to pick up the baby. Then, she let out a piercing scream that made my blood turn to ice.

In Erica's hands was not a human baby but some kind of grotesque gnome baby. It was greenish brown, dotted with huge warts, and had patches of coarse, black hair sprouting in all kinds of unlikely places. It looked into Erica's eyes and smiled, showing rows of tiny pointed teeth. We heard footsteps charging up the stairs. The human baby's parents must have heard Erica scream.

"The Spriggan switched the babies," Erica shrieked.

"Take that thing!" I said quickly. "The parents will have heart attacks if they see it in the crib!"

Maybe if we hurried, I thought quickly, we could get the real baby back before her parents came into the room. After all, Fairyland time was only a few seconds of human time.

Erica took the baby and jumped back into the picture. I grabbed the baby carrier, so she wouldn't have to hold the awful baby, and we followed. On the way out, Katrina pointed her finger and zapped. We landed on the hill, and the picture, now shrunken to its normal size, fell to the ground.

"We don't want the baby's parents running all over Fairyland, do we?" said Katrina as I picked up the picture.

"I guess not," I said uneasily.

I held up the baby carrier. "Here, Erica," I said. "Put that gross thing in this. Maybe we can leave him over here by this tree."

The fairies were appalled. They seemed to think it ghastly to leave a baby, however horrible, alone and unprotected. They complained so much that Erica finally put the baby carrier on her back.

"Toss him in here," she said resignedly, passing the baby to me.

The little Spriggan was screaming and crying, like a

human baby but much louder. He tried to bite me as I placed him in the baby carrier. He leaned over Erica's shoulder and blew hot, smelly breath on her face. Then, he noticed Erica's baby Joy Fairy playing on its swing. The little Spriggan smiled. The baby fairy was delighted to play with someone his own age. They kept each other busy, and we all caught our breath.

We saw a small figure coming toward us. It was Mab, followed by a large group of fairies of all sizes, including the dwarf, who looked as if he had told Mab of Erica's plan. Mab was still a little taller than me, even outside the Fairy Court, so I guess she was a fairy who could change her height when it was needed.

Erica spoke first. "The baby has been taken by the Spriggan. This," she showed the horrid baby and everyone gasped, "was left in its place!"

Mab looked fierce. "Then it's war on the Shadow Forces. I must contact the Queen. She will try to prevent the Empress from leaving her court."

"Please, wait!" I said. "What about Annie? She's disappeared and might be in danger!"

Mab thought for a moment. "Our informant told us that the Spriggan's plan was to take the baby to the castle of the Giant. Because the Spriggan guards the Giant's treasure, the Giant will give him refuge for the night. We must get the child from the Spriggan tonight, before he leaves the Giant's castle. If the baby is brought before the Empress Varinka, we may never get her back!"

"You girls must band together, with all your fairies and these court fairies who have agreed to help their Queen in case of emergencies like this. Make the Spriggan tell you what he did with Annie. Force him to return the child. And please, be careful, since the Spriggan might harm the baby if you try to harm him.

"Erica, you must lead the fairies. You know the most about the Spriggan, and the Giant. Please remember, however, you cannot do everything yourself. Rebecca and these fairies are here to help you. Use them wisely, and you cannot fail."

The fairies let out a tremendous cheer. Erica stood tall and proud, her baby Spriggan drooling on her shoulder.

❧ 18 ❧

Giant's Castle

Erica didn't waste a moment. "Everyone, follow me to the Giant's castle," she shouted. Her ring grew to the size of a doorway, and with fairies holding our hands, and clinging to almost every part of us, we stepped through.

"What's your plan, General?" I asked Erica.

"First thing I plan to do is to get rid of this baby Spriggan," she said crossly. "He's starting to get heavy."

The horrid baby had already grown quite a bit since we first saw him. Spriggans must grow at a much different rate than human babies. His teeth were bigger, too.

Erica put us all in a circle and outlined her plan.

"We need to find a way into the Giant's castle, and we need to find where he keeps his gold. That would be the safest, most familiar place for the Spriggan. Is there a fairy here with the power to enter forbidden places?"

A fairy no bigger than a hummingbird fluttered in front of Erica and raised her hand.

"Are there any fairies that can bewitch with their dancing?"

Several twinkling, long-legged fairies leaped over and volunteered.

"How about a fairy who has the power to reveal secrets?"

Another fairy, who looked like a small, delicate woman, stepped forward.

"Any sleep fairies?"

A group of tiny fairies, showering down like a handful of confetti, landed in a group next to Erica.

"All right," Erica said, "here's the plan. This fairy," she pointed to the hummingbird-sized one, "will enter the castle and open the lock on one of the doors. The Giant will be angry when he sees her, so the dancing fairies will slide in and bewitch the Giant with their dancing. Once he's pretty dazed, the secret fairy will get the Giant to reveal where the gold is hidden. The sleep fairies will then put the Giant to sleep."

"What about the Spriggan?" I asked.

"He'll be near the gold. Then, it's a simple matter of frightening him by turning my clothes inside out. When he screams and hides his eyes, I'll grab the baby, and we'll dash out of there."

"What about Annie?" I asked again.

"I'll have to see when we get to the Spriggan," said

Erica uncertainly. "Perhaps he's holding her prisoner. Or maybe—"

"Or maybe what?" I asked, not really wanting to hear the answer.

"The Giant might have eaten her by now," she said, wincing.

There was a tense silence. None of us wanted to think about that.

"Let's get going," Erica said. The fairies were starting to get excited about saving the baby and showing off their magic to each other. Erica had found a job for nearly every fairy there. She stepped over to me, taking the baby carrier off her shoulders and handing it to me.

"You have a very important job, Rebecca," she said. "You must watch the baby Spriggan while we're in the castle. Stay here and wait for us."

She couldn't be serious!

"Why do I need to watch the baby Spriggan? I want to go in the castle with you!"

Erica sighed. "We need fairies that have certain powers. We don't need Katrina. It's simply not a job for a counter-fairy."

Katrina went crazy. She went straight for Erica's hair and starting pulling on it. It took several fairies to pull her off. One of the larger fairies put the screaming and kicking Katrina in my hands. Then, Erica and the fairies marched off without me. They left me with a smelly baby Spriggan in one hand and a shrieking fairy in the other.

I let go of Katrina when Erica was out of sight. She flew straight over to Merridie to complain.

"That straw-haired witch!" she cried. "One day she will know what my powers can do!" Merridie put a friendly hand on Katrina's shoulder and they embraced.

I felt bad for Katrina but worse for myself. Here I was again; back to being the one left out of everything. Fairyland looked more like the human world every moment I was here.

The baby Spriggan was kicking up such a commotion that I had to set him down on the ground. He looked up at me with his piggy little eyes and started sniffling. The fairies fluttered in front of his face, trying to cheer him up. Then he started crying again. He rubbed his eyes with his knobby little fists, and fell over sideways. I reached over to pick him up, and he snapped at me.

"Suit yourself, Junior," I said.

Katrina flew over. "Junior is his name?"

"Sure," I said sulkily. "Why not?"

"Junior, Junior," the fairies sang, trying to amuse him.

He was not amused. Inside of smiling, he got up on

all fours and started crawling away. He stopped for a moment, and seemed to listen to something. Then, he started crawling faster. Junior was heading straight for the Giant's castle.

"Do you think he knows his father is in there?" I asked Katrina. She smiled and winked at me.

It was a dilemma. Erica said to watch the baby Spriggan. If I followed him, I was still watching him. She also said to stay here and wait. If I couldn't do both things at once, I decided I would do what she said first.

I told Merridie that she didn't have to come with us, but she insisted on staying with Katrina. They were now best friends, since Merridie took Katrina's part in the argument with Erica. Merridie also wanted to find out what happened to the baby.

Junior crawled up to a dark side of the castle. I could make out a high wall. Water splashed behind it, so I assumed there was a moat surrounding the castle. We weren't going to get over that wall unless it was by magic.

"What are Merridie's powers?" I whispered to Katrina.

"You saw them," she said simply.

What does that mean? I thought. Then Junior started crawling fast along the wall, toward a big object. When the clouds moved past the moon, I saw that it was a pipe.

Katrina flew over the wall to see where it led. It turned out to go under the moat and, apparently, right into the castle. Junior looked over his shoulder at me and grinned mischievously with his pointy little teeth.

19

Junior

It must have been a sewage pipe, because it smelled perfectly awful. If Junior had been anything other than a baby Spriggan, I wouldn't have let him crawl through it. As it was, I had to crawl through it, too. Katrina and Merridie flew through it, but they still found it disgusting, and, of course, they complained the entire way.

There was a faint light at the end of the pipe. When we reached it, it led to a kind of underground canal. The pipe, I guessed, helped drain the water out of the canal when it overflowed. Overflowed with what, I didn't want to imagine. Bones kept floating by at regular intervals. There were torches attached to the walls, and they dimly lit the way. Junior decided to crawl along the side of the canal. The ledge was very shallow; only about a foot wide. I edged along sideways with my back against the wall, trying not to look into the murky waters below. Strangely, I felt a little worried about Junior and hoped he wouldn't fall in the water. I didn't know if I was starting to like him, or if I just wanted him to lead me to his father. Probably both, I decided.

We traveled that way for a long time. Then, I heard the sound of oars slapping the water. Someone in a boat was heading in our direction. There was a recess in the wall about ten yards ahead. If I could get to it, maybe we wouldn't be seen. The fairies flew ahead to the recess and hid. I scooped Junior up and started shuffling sideways along the wall. Junior was not at all happy with me, since my hand was firmly over his mouth. His head squirmed from side to side. His body was wiggling madly. He was trying to bite me, and it was a miracle that I didn't drop him in the water. I reached the recess just in time.

Two trolls were chatting in the boat.

"Do you hear something sniffling?"

"No. You're mad. You're starting to get old and daft."

"The master is getting daft. The upstairs house troll told me that the master has dancing girls in tonight!"

"You don't say! Didn't know he liked that sort of thing!"

They rowed on, and I couldn't hear the rest of their conversation.

At least I knew that Erica's plan had worked up to the dancing fairy point. I put Junior down on the ledge again, and he happily crawled away.

Soon, we reached a larger recess in the wall of the canal. It had a spiral staircase in it, and Junior started making his way up the stairs. What I soon found out was this: Spriggans are very good climbers. They have long fingers and toes like monkeys. Junior was climbing so quickly, even the fairies were having a hard time keeping up with him, and they were *flying*! We went up about eight stories high and came to a landing and a wall.

There was no floor on the landing, just the little space at the top of the stairs. I could see the light of a room shining through a window in the wall about twenty feet away to my left, but there seemed to be no way to get to it. I looked up. There were metal bars in the ceiling above me, spaced about a foot and a half apart. Junior started whimpering, and I picked him up. I reached up to grab one of the bars. I held it in my hand for a second, and then it disappeared! I nearly lost my balance. Katrina flew over to have a look.

"Enchanted," she said simply. She snapped her fingers twice. "Try them now," she said.

I put my hand up. The bar was solid. "Thanks, Katrina," I said gratefully. I held Junior in my hands and looked at him.

"If you want to see your daddy, Junior, you're going to have to come with me. Hold on to my back and don't let go. Don't look down either." He must have understood me, because he immediately looked down. Terrified, he scampered onto my back and gripped my neck tightly. His fingernails were digging into my skin, but it was hard to be mad at him—he was a warty baby, but still a baby.

I reached up to the bar. I jumped a little and grabbed on with the other hand. Swinging myself eight stories high, I thought I couldn't possibly make it across. I told Katrina and Merridie to fly ahead and see what was waiting for us there. I slowly started moving, swinging very carefully. Junior was babbling now in some weird Spriggan baby language, and he was shaking like a leaf. My arms were starting to hurt, and my hands were getting moist. It was hard to get a good grip. The light was getting brighter, then Katrina and Merridie flew up.

"You are not going to believe your eyes," said Katrina helpfully.

I swung off the last bar through the window into the brightly lit room. The reason the room was so bright was that it was filled from floor to ceiling with gold! Junior dropped off my back and started crawling toward the far wall. Halfway there, he pushed himself up onto his feet and took his first steps! He was now officially a toddler. He turned a hidden corner quickly, and I chased after him. Then, I heard a familiar shriek.

It was Erica. She was alone, except for her Joy Fairy.

She was outside of a door with a little barred window. Junior was reaching out to the Joy Fairy. He wanted to play! Erica, however, was not in a playing mood. Her gown was inside out, but I didn't see the Spriggan anywhere.

"How is the plan coming along?" I asked her. "Where are the other fairies?"

She looked really forlorn. "I sent them back. It was too dangerous for us all to be in the castle. I wanted to get them out while the Giant was asleep."

Katrina fluttered in. "We know where our Spriggan is, Erica. Where is yours?"

She nodded her head toward the door. I peered in. What I saw frightened me down to the tips of my toes.

20

Rescue

There was the Spriggan. I had imagined that he would look like a bigger version of Junior, but I was wrong. He was terrifying. His hairy body hunched over, and his arms hung down almost to the ground. When he yawned, I noticed his sharp yellow teeth and long black tongue. His eyes were also yellow, and he had only a hole where his nose should have been. When he saw me, he puffed himself up to twice his original size. I almost jumped out of my skin! The most frightening thing about him, however, was the way he was holding the human baby.

He had her by the feet and was holding her upside down. If we tried to get at him, he would drop her on her head. She was (understandably) crying loudly. Then I noticed something in the corner of the room. It was Annie, and she was tied up. Her fairy Brianna was floating next to the Spriggan. I tried the handle on the door. It was locked.

"What happened?" I asked Erica.

Erica leaned forward and whispered. "The Spriggan already had the baby. He was waiting for Annie when she came to protect her. He knew she would bring a powerful fairy, like Brianna. If he threatened the baby, he knew he could force Annie to give control of Brianna to him. He left his baby in place of the other to fool us into thinking the baby was safe!"

Like we wouldn't be able to tell the difference, I thought, glancing over at Junior.

"The Spriggan used Brianna to make a shield to protect him from any kind of magic. Then, he ordered one of the Giant's servants to take a message to the Empress Varinka. She's coming here to collect the baby herself!"

Erica continued in a sad voice. "When I got here, I thought I could scare the Spriggan by turning my gown inside out," she said. "When I saw that that wouldn't work, because of the protection spell, I sent Violet to get help. But I don't think anyone will get here in time."

Suddenly, we heard angry noises downstairs.

"The Giant must be awake now," said Erica. "We have to do something quickly. When he lets the Empress in, she'll take the baby, and leave *us* to the Giant."

I thought of the bones floating in the canal. Then I remembered something important.

"If we get through Brianna's shield, then we can scare the Spriggan, right?" I asked Erica.

"Yes, but he'll drop the baby on her head," she pointed out.

I looked at Katrina. She looked at me very seriously. Our eyes met in a kind of unspoken understanding.

She quickly flew through the barred window and unlocked the door. I opened the door the tiniest crack, so as not to startle the Spriggan.

Erica hissed, "What are you doing?"

I shushed her. Carefully, I pushed Junior through the crack in the door.

It was actually kind of sweet. Junior held out his little arms, just like a human baby, and toddled over to the Spriggan. The Spriggan, however, was completely bewildered. How did the baby he left in the human world make it all the way back to him? Confused, he cautiously put the human baby down. At that moment, Katrina and I pushed the door completely open. In a split second, Katrina zapped the magic shield from the Spriggan, and he was completely unprotected.

I looked immediately for Merridie. She was flying by Katrina's side, unaware of my intentions for her. I snatched her quickly and threw her hard at the Spriggan. She turned into pond water in midair and landed right in the Spriggan's face. He screamed in agony, and Junior started crying. I dashed over to Annie and untied her. Erica scooped up the baby girl.

We heard the sound of footsteps approaching. The Empress must have arrived for the baby! I tried to think clearly, but nothing came to mind.

"Where did you tell Violet to meet you?" I asked Erica, quickly.

"In the counting room," Erica replied. "It's across the hall to the right."

Merridie flew out of the Spriggan's eyes and joined us as we exited the room. The Spriggan was still reeling around, and we locked him in the room as we left. We piled into the counting room and locked that door. Erica stuck her finger in the baby's mouth so that she could suck on it quietly.

I opened the window and looked out. There was no sign of Violet. There was nothing we could do but wait.

I could hear the steps of the Empress drawing closer. Peeking out of the keyhole, I caught a glimpse of her as she strode past. She had a magnificent chiseled beauty, but her face looked hard and angry. Her clothes, made of a satiny material, were all bright red. Katrina informed me that rumor was that the cloth was dyed with the blood of the Empress's victims! My heart jumped into my throat.

We tried to listen to the Empress Varinka questioning

the Spriggan. The problem was that Junior was shrieking his head off about something. Maybe he was trying to help us, because every time the Empress or the Spriggan spoke, Junior would yell at the top of his lungs. I thought I heard her say something like, "Have you lost the other as well?" but I couldn't be sure.

Suddenly, Violet flew into the room. She pointed outside, and there, leading up to the window, was a roadway in the air—a fairy roadway! It started at the windowsill and continued right up into the sky. It was lit with tiny colored lights on each side of it, but the surface of it was almost invisible. It looked like light purple mist.

"Let's go," I said.

Erica went out first with the baby, followed by Annie. The doorknob of the room started jiggling. I motioned for the fairies to leave, but they refused to move until I jumped on the windowsill. The door burst open right then, and the Empress Varinka, the Spriggan, and Junior all charged in. I looked down at the purple mist and stepped out. It seemed solid enough, so I took off, running. The fairies were right behind me.

Empress Varinka roared in outrage. When I turned to look at her, she was stepping onto the roadway. Katrina whirled around and pointed her finger at the road. *Zap!* The Empress fell through the purple mist into the moat below. The Spriggan now had no way of following us. He shook his fist at me in frustration. I waved good-bye to Junior, who was standing on the windowsill. He opened and closed his long fingers in a bye-bye gesture. Then he bit his dad's arm.

21

Fairy Queen

I dashed up the roadway after the others. The Empress recovered quickly from her fall; she was rising up from the moat on the back of a colossal water beast! It had enormous wings, and the head of a lion, but the tail of a fish. Varinka held its wet mane in her hands like reins, and commanded it to destroy us.

Annie screamed, "Get between that thing and us, Brianna!" and she launched her fairy hard at the beast.

From the beast's mouth, one steady stream of blue flame came at us. But Brianna bravely shielded us, and the flames bounced off her and back into the monster's face. It howled in pain and dove with its mouth wide open back into the moat. For now, Varinka was vanquished! But I had a feeling that wasn't the last we'd seen of her.

Suddenly, we came to the top of a peak in the roadway. Erica stopped and looked down.

"I'd better sit down for this," she said, adjusting the baby on her lap.

Then, she disappeared. One by one, we climbed to the top. When I got there, I realized why everyone was disappearing. The roadway was pointing straight down.

I sat down and pretended that I was at the top of a very high slide. Katrina decided to grab onto my hair, and Merridie joined her. I closed my eyes and pushed off.

The air went rushing by like a huge fan was blowing on me. I felt myself dropping and dropping, until I thought it would never stop. The roadway twisted and turned, and at one point, formed a complete corkscrew! Then, suddenly, I landed.

The end of the roadway led into a pile of huge feather cushions on the floor of the Fairy Court. The court members were back, and they were applauding wildly. Annie helped me to my feet. I returned her picture frame to her. The crowd parted, and I saw Erica, triumphantly holding the baby in the air. On one side of her stood Mab. On her other side was the most majestic fairy I'd ever seen. Her sharp green eyes took in the whole scene, and she smiled warmly at us. Her gown was made of white silk and was decorated with ribbons of gold that seemed to be moving in twists and circles all around the sleeves and bodice. On her head, she wore a crown, which changed color dramatically as she turned her head. This must be the Fairy Queen.

Katrina and Merridie let go of my hair. I noticed that

they were still normal fairy size. The Fairy Court's magic kept them tiny. It was a good thing, too. I was used to them that way.

The Queen was holding up her hands for silence. The applause stopped immediately.

"I wish to make a speech tonight. We have a great deal to be thankful for this evening. Our girls and fairies have shown their bravery in many ways. They must all be commended. Will each of you step forward?"

She introduced each fairy who helped Erica storm the Giant's castle. To each fairy, she bestowed a kiss on the forehead, and a gift, wrapped in gold paper. The Queen turned back to the crowd.

"Now, I must give special thanks to Annie, who suffered greatly through a terrible ordeal. Please come forward and collect your reward."

Annie had an enormous smile on her face as she marched proudly up to the Queen. She knelt before her, collecting her gift, as did her fairies, Thalia and Brianna, who were joyously flying in circles around her head.

"The Queen Mother tells me that there was one girl in charge of the mission tonight. Her coordination of the fairies was extraordinary. Let us all give our thanks to Erica!"

A tremendous roar went up in the crowd, and I spied

the dwarf gatekeeper near the back of the room. He was clapping as loudly as anyone else, as Erica knelt before the Queen.

The Queen lifted Erica's face, and kissed her on the forehead. Then, she tickled the baby fairy near Erica's ear. Violet flew up alongside Erica, and the Queen gently kissed her as well. Erica leaned over and whispered something in the Queen's ear.

"Erica tells me that there is one girl and two fairies responsible for the complete success of this mission. The girl has not been with us long, but she has already made her mark. For their outstanding contribution to the baby's rescue, I ask you all to thank Rebecca, Katrina, and Merridie!"

My face was red hot. I felt as if I were glued to the spot. Katrina and Merridie both took my hands and dragged me up before the Queen. We all knelt before her, even Katrina. I never thought she would kneel before anyone! The Queen kissed us and gave us our gifts.

"Rebecca, you are now one of us. Please accept my personal thanks and my admiration for your bravery," the Queen added. Then, she bowed before me!

My eyes darted over to Katrina, who gave me a look she had never given me before. It was a look of respect. I whispered the words, "Thank you."

22

Rewards

"Now, everyone, join me in a celebration!" said the Queen. She led the way into the Great Dining Hall, where a special feast covered the tables.

I didn't think it polite to open my present right away. Apparently, Katrina did not agree. She and Merridie tore theirs open immediately. Merridie received a necklace made completely of live glowworms, which she wore proudly all night long. Katrina received the deed to a home of her own, close to the castle.

"I know the place well, and it's a very good neighborhood," I heard her confide to Merridie. "But the place itself is small and cramped. And, of course, there are *blue jays* living directly above. You know how *that* is!"

Merridie and Katrina both rolled their eyes.

The feast began, but I didn't see Annie until it was almost over. When I asked where she had gone, she told me that the Queen asked her to put the baby back in its crib.

"She's protected now. The Queen put an enchantment on her that the Shadow Forces can't reverse. It will last until she's our age. Her parents didn't even know she was gone!"

It was a wonderful feast, with plenty of fairy entertainment. Everyone had their favorite performers. Annie loved the fairy acrobats. Erica admired the chorus of fairy singers. I asked Katrina which act she enjoyed. She confided that she most enjoyed the fairy magician, who could turn mice into miniature horses and pebbles and beads into precious gems.

"Turning rocks into jewels!" she crowed, "Now that's one enchantment I would never undo!"

I most enjoyed the way the members of the Fairy Court came up to me and introduced themselves. Fairies, elves, imps, and dwarfs greeted me and thanked me all through the feast. My cheeks and forehead must have been kissed a thousand times!

Before dessert, we were told to open our gifts. Mine was a rectangular object, made of gold, about the size of my palm. In the center was a screen, with little twisting wormlike images moving around it. At first, I thought they were alive. Then, I saw that if I moved my hand and pointed the object toward a fairy, the wormlike images formed words. I pointed it at Merridie.

"It's an Indicator!" Erica squealed when she saw my gift. "This is wonderful! Now you'll never have to listen to another lecture from me!"

Erica showed me her gift. It was a beautifully illustrated book entitled <u>The Guide to the Etiquette of Fairyland: How to Open the Doors of Communication</u>.

She had to laugh. "I think the Queen is dropping a large hint with this gift!"

Annie's gift was as amazing as mine. It looked like a large marble. Inside it, blue liquid was swirling and churning. When she held in up to her face and whispered the name of one of her fairies, the liquid cleared, and she could see the face of the fairy. When she spoke, her fairy could speak back to her! It was like a fairy telephone!

"Now I can talk to them whenever I like!" she said happily. "I really miss them when I'm in the real world."

The real world! I tried to calculate what time it was back in my house. My mom would be home right now. She probably wouldn't miss me, but she might notice the books Katrina threw out the window. One of them landed right on top of her rhododendrons. It was time to leave Fairyland.

I exchanged good-bye kisses with Annie and Erica and all of their fairies. We promised to meet again soon, when we returned for our next assignments.

Katrina and Merridie did not want me to go without them! Katrina had promised Merridie that she could see her glamorous new home in the human world. I had to be very stern.

"I will bring you both with me on our next mission," I promised.

"Don't touch a thing in my house in the human realm," Katrina commanded, and I promised to leave it exactly as she left it.

"Then perhaps we can work together, sometimes," she conceded, and flew off, Merridie trailing behind.

I wanted to say a special good-bye to Mab.

"Thank you for believing in me," I said sincerely. "It's really amazing that you did! I didn't even believe in myself!"

Mab hugged me. "I saw the gift in you right away," she said simply. "That's *my* special power!"

I left the court via express water sprite and stepped through the center of the watch face. From the garden, I could see my mom in the kitchen. From the way she was slamming the cupboard doors, and smacking things down on the counter, I could see she was in a major snit about something.

Opening the sliding doors, I strolled casually into the kitchen. She turned to me with a look of pure fury.

"WHY is there an orange lizard swimming in my $3,000 crystal punch bowl?"

"It's a salamander, Mom," I replied. "It's an amphibian, not a lizard."

"Where did it come from, may I ask?" she said, placing her hands on her hips. She hated to be corrected.

I looked at the faint pink mark on my right forearm. "From me, Mom," I said truthfully. "From me and Jenny Greenteeth."

She looked at me hard. She looked at me as if I was a difficult puzzle she would need years and years to figure out. That look was worth everything.